"Well, it was nice to have met you,"

Emma told Adam, reverting out of sheer nervousness to the overly proper way she used to talk. She reached her hand out to Adam automatically.

As the other girls started toward the hotel, Adam took her hand. "Nice to have met you, too," he said softly. "Now, find some way to come back out here. I'll be waiting by that corner." He indicated the intersection of California and Pine streets with his eyes.

Emma's heart pounded in her chest. "I can't do that!" she whispered.

"I'll be waiting," he said in a low voice.

The SUNSET ISLAND series
by Cherie Bennett

Sunset Island
Sunset Kiss
Sunset Dreams
Sunset Farewell
Sunset Reunion
Sunset Secrets
Sunset Heat
Sunset Promises
Sunset Scandal
Sunset Whispers
Sunset Paradise

Also created by Cherie Bennett

Sunset After Dark
Sunset After Midnight
Sunset After Hours

Sunset Surf

CHERIE BENNETT

SPLASH™

B

A BERKLEY / SPLASH BOOK

SUNSET SURF is an original publication of
The Berkley Publishing Group.
This work has never appeared before in book form.

SUNSET SURF

A Berkley Book / published by arrangement with
General Licensing Company, Inc.

PRINTING HISTORY
Berkley edition / May 1993

A GLC BOOK

Splash is a trademark belonging to General Licensing
Company, Inc.

ISBN: 0-425-13937-9

A BERKLEY BOOK ® TM 757,375
Berkley Books are published by The Berkley Publishing Group,
200 Madison Avenue, New York, New York 10016.
The name "BERKLEY" and the "B" logo
are trademarks belonging to Berkley Publishing Corporation.

PRINTED IN THE UNITED STATES OF AMERICA

10 9 8 7 6 5 4 3 2 1

—As always, for Jeff—

ONE

"Are we winning yet?" Samantha Bridges asked her boyfriend, Presley Travis, squinting at the scoreboards some volunteers were posting near the judges' table.

"No, we're not winning," Pres replied in his sexy Tennessee drawl, "and we ain't likely to if you keep on eating while we're supposed to be competing!"

"Oh, lighten up," Sam told him with a laugh. She shoved her hot dog in his face and he good-naturedly took a huge bite.

"The second-to-last event in the first annual COPE Sunset Island Couples Olympics," a tinny voice boomed out over the makeshift sound system set up on the main beach at Sunset Island, "is the Soda Bottle Fill. All couples entered in this event please proceed to the staging area in

1

ten minutes. Howie, quit tickling me!" Molly Mason, who was seated at the judges' table, jokingly poked back at Howie Lawrence as she finished her announcement. The crowd of about a hundred teens and on-lookers laughed heartily.

Pres walked over to Billy Sampson to tell him something, and Sam sidled over next to her best friends, Carrie Alden and Emma Cresswell. She watched Pres walk away and nodded appreciatively. "That boy is filled with talent, isn't he?"

Carrie laughed. "I have a feeling you're not referring to how well he plays the bass."

"You got that right," Sam agreed with a smirk, swallowing the last of her hot dog.

Emma nudged Sam in the ribs. "Do you ever think about anything besides sex and food?" she asked teasingly.

"Of course," Sam said with dignity. "Fashion."

"She's hopeless!" Carrie exclaimed, but it was obvious she didn't really mean it.

"You love me and you know it," Sam said, beaming at Emma and Carrie. Like Sam, Emma and Carrie were dressed in long T-shirts that read, "COPE: The Future of Sunset Island." *I am so lucky to have them as my best friends,* Sam thought to herself. She thought back to the day they'd met at the International Au Pair Convention in New York City the previous year. They'd become fast friends and were thrilled when they'd all landed jobs as au pairs on fabulous Sunset Island, a ritzy summer resort off the coast of Maine. They'd been an odd trio right from the start—tall, redheaded, outrageous Sam from small-town Kansas with dreams of becoming rich and famous; Boston heiress Emma with her perfect blond bob and European education; and intelligent, cause-joining, girl-next-door Carrie. But somehow the combination worked, and now Sam couldn't imagine her life without Emma and Carrie in it.

We are living proof that you don't have to be the same as your friends in order to be friends, Sam thought happily.

"This Couple Olympics thing was a great idea," Carrie said, watching Molly and Howie adding up some scores before they started the next event. "I hope we raise tons of money for COPE. It's such a good idea, I wish I'd thought of it."

"Well, you didn't," Sam said with a smile,

looking over at Pres again. "Emma did. Right, Emma?"

Emma shrugged, and sipped a cup of water. "I didn't exactly think of it all by myself. It sort of was a group decision, at the last COPE meeting."

Emma had been introduced to an activist group called COPE—Citizens of Positive Ethics—by her boyfriend, Kurt Ackerman, who lived on the island year-round. Originally formed to stop unscrupulous developers from turning an ecologically-sensitive area of the island into time-share condominiums, lately COPE had been focusing its efforts on disaster relief—after Hurricane Julius had slammed into the island earlier in the summer and had left many island residents homeless.

"Listen. It's extremely cool that Pres and I might win the fancy dinner for two at the Sunset Inn, but know what I think the coolest part of this is?" Sam asked her friends. She looked over at the judges' table where Howie and Molly had their heads close together, deep in discussion. "It's the budding COPE romance underway at the judges' table."

"They really do seem to like each other,"

4

Emma agreed. "I think it's great. I remember when Darcy couldn't get Molly out of the house on the hill."

"Me too," Carrie said, smiling at Molly, who was laughing at something Howie said.

"Me three," said Sam. She spotted a tall, muscular girl with gorgeous long, thick black hair over the heads of a bunch of people. "Hey Darcy!" Sam called and waved her over.

"She's probably winning," Emma said. "She's a great athlete." Emma watched Darcy as she walked across the sand.

Wow, Darcy looks great, Emma thought. *She's probably the fittest girl I know. Look at her muscles!* She had met Darcy one day when she was going door to door in a post-hurricane solicitation for COPE. Darcy, it turned out, had been hired by Molly Mason's parents to take care of Molly following the auto accident that had left spunky Molly confined to a wheelchair. Darcy had gotten to be really good friends with Emma, Sam and Carrie. It was largely because of Darcy that Molly was able to begin to emerge from her depression and

5

even show up at an event like the Couple Olympics.

"What do you think of the budding romance?" Sam asked Darcy with a grin, jerking her head meaningfully toward Molly and Howie.

"Pretty cool," Darcy said to her lightly. "But I think Molly can do better than Howie Lawrence."

Emma and Carrie groaned. "Howie Lawrence is a really nice guy and a really good friend," Carrie said in Howie's defense.

"Yeah, he's a nice guy," Sam agreed. "But until recently he also had the world's biggest crush on a certain Ivory-girl type from New Jersey, so basically you're just glad he's glommed on to someone else!"

"Not fair!" Carrie cried out.

"Well, you know what I always say," Sam began. "If you're not going to be a tall, dark, handsome rich guy, you may as well just be rich like Howie." With that, Sam rubbed her thumb against her other fingers, indicating *money.*

"That is so crass," Carrie said, wincing. *Howie Lawrence* is *a really nice guy,*

Emma thought to herself. *He can't help it if he was born a little nerdy-looking, and . . .*

"Very rich!" Darcy smiled, looking right at Emma as if she knew exactly what Emma was thinking, but replying to what Sam had said. *Darcy amazes me,* Emma thought. *It's like sometimes she can read exactly what's in my mind.*

Emma looked at Darcy. "How did you know what I was—"

Darcy cut her off with a wink and a wave. "I see the guys over by the staging area," she said. "We'd all better get over to the next event."

"Try not to detour to the food tables," Emma told Sam, pointing her in the right direction.

Now, these are some seriously cute guys, Sam thought to herself appreciatively as they walked over to the staging area. In addition to Pres there was Billy Sampson, lead singer for the up-and-coming rock band Flirting With Danger. Billy and Carrie were a major league item. There was also Emma's swim-instructor boyfriend, Kurt Ackerman. And there was a tall, muscular musician friend of Pres's from Tennessee, Wyatt James, who had the bluest eyes the girls had ever seen and who was competing as Darcy Laken's partner.

The volunteers finally got the scores up, and Sam pointed to the sign. "Darcy and Wyatt are winning. Not for long!"

"We'll see about that," Darcy said with a grin.

"Okay, listen up," Molly Mason's voice boomed out over the loudspeakers. The crowd hushed.

"This event is the Soda Bottle Fill," Molly continued loudly. "Each couple starts with a beach bucket full of water, a teaspoon and a twelve-ounce soda bottle. The guys take water out of the bucket with the teaspoon and hand it to the girls, who then pour it into the soda bottles. First couple that holds a full bottle up in the air is the winner. Any questions?" Molly paused expectantly.

"Even Lorell Courtland could figure this one," Sam whispered loudly. She was referring to one of the girls' two arch-enemies on the island. Lorell and her buddy, Diana De Witt, seemed to make their lifes' purpose making these girls miserable. To make things worse, Diana had managed to land one of the three backup singer slots with

Flirting With Danger. So now Emma, Sam and Diana were actually in the same band!

"Shhh!" Emma whispered back.

Molly's voice boomed out again. "Five points for first place, three for second, one for third. All couples ready? Okay, start when the gun fires!" At this point, Howie Lawrence took out a starter pistol and pointed it skyward.

CRACK! All the couples started madly trying to fill their soda bottles. But it seemed like more water was being spilled on the beach than actually made it into the bottles. The crowd rooted and cheered and most of the contestants were laughing more than they were competing. Kurt and Emma, though, worked smoothly as a team, and it seemed like only seconds before they both took hold of their bottle and thrust it into the air. They were followed quickly by Butchie Gleason and Susan Perkins, two Sunset Island locals who had friends who lost property in the hurricane, and Darcy and Wyatt.

Howie Lawrence whistled the event to a stop.

"We have a winner!" Molly Mason sang out over the public address system. "It's the team of Kurt Ackerman and Emma Cresswell. The standings, going into the last event, are Darcy Laken and Wyatt James with twenty-four points, Ackerman and Cresswell with twenty-two, and three different couples are tied at eighteen points!"

"We're in third place and there's only one event left!" Sam exclaimed, punching Pres in the arm. "We were supposed to win this sucker!"

"I'll make it up to you somehow," Pres teased, putting his arms around Sam.

"Way to go, Kurt and Emma!" Ethan Hewitt yelled from the crowd. Twelve-year-old Ethan was the oldest of the three kids that Emma baby-sat for.

A cheer went up for Kurt and Emma. Everyone joined in except for two slim girls in bikinis who were standing off to the side watching the proceedings with supercilious looks on their faces. They booed.

"It's Diana and Lorell," Carrie groaned.

"When will those girls get a clue?" Sam asked rhetorically.

"Probably never," Darcy said matter-of-factly.

As if to confirm Darcy's feelings, Lorell's

10

voice rang out to them. "Oh Sammie," she cooed in her syrupy Georgia drawl, "does fillin' pop bottles with water make you and your do-good friends feel better?"

"It does, Lorell," Sam shot back. "But not as good as I would feel if you'd, like, go for a swim in the ocean and try to make it over to Europe."

Lorell and Diana gave mock laughs. "Oooh, isn't the girl from Kansas clever!" Lorell continued. "Well, I'm sure the five-hundred dollars this event is going to raise for COPE is going to put every one of those poor people back in their homes!"

"It's a start," Carrie said emphatically, drawing close to Sam's side.

"Not much of one," Diana said, archly. Sam started to retort, but Emma took hold of her arm.

"Don't let them wind you up," Emma whispered. "We're doing something important. Come on. Let's get out of here." Sam nodded her head to Emma and turned away. But she couldn't resist just one parting shot at Diana and Lorell.

"Guess you couldn't find someone to enter with, Diana," Sam said sweetly. "That

11

must be what happens after you sleep with every guy in Maine."

"Not your guy," Diana called after her. "Not yet, anyway."

"Ignore her," Carrie advised Sam, putting her hand lightly on Sam's arm.

"Okay, Olympians, it's time for the final event!" Molly called out over the sound system. "The Water Balloon Toss!"

Molly explained the rules: each couple would get a water balloon, all the guys would line up in one line, all the girls in another, and each couple would throw the balloons back and forth taking a step back after each completed throw. The couple that could throw and catch the balloon from the farthest distance without breaking it, would earn eight points.

"It's kind of like a wet T-shirt contest!" someone in the crowd yelled out.

"Well, that means Sam will lose for sure!" Diana yelled.

Sam turned bright red at this nasty reference to her small bustline. "I have to kill her," she muttered under her breath.

"She's not worth the jail time," Emma said gently.

"I don't know," Sam mused. "The longer

I know her and Lorell, the more I think I'd be doing humanity a favor if I offed them both. No jury would find me guilty."

"Places, please!" Molly called.

All the couples lined up, and again Howie Lawrence blasted away with his starter pistol. Multi-colored water balloons filled the air. Most couples dropped out quickly, and many people were soaked—but laughing— after the balloons burst in their grasping hands. Carrie, who was normally very sure-handed, shrieked when a bobbled catch soaked her from head to toe.

Within four minutes, only three couples were left: Emma and Kurt, Darcy and Wyatt, Butchie and Susan. Then Darcy made a throw that Wyatt bobbled and dropped. Just two couples left! They went throw for throw for another minute, and then Susan threw one to Butchie that erupted in midair. Kurt and Emma had won the Olympics!

There was lots of cheering, and the two of them took some good-natured ribbing because everyone knew that Emma and Kurt were both pretty involved with COPE. But Molly and Howie ruled that they had won fair and square. And they awarded the two the certificate good for dinner at the Sunset Inn, the most chic restaurant in town.

"Yeah, like you needed to win a free dinner," Sam groused to Emma.

"Now, Sam, be a good sport," Carrie admonished Sam.

"But she just won a trip to Paradise Island a few weeks ago!" Sam reminded Carrie. "Was she born under a lucky star or what?"

"Hey, Emma's had to deal with a lot of crap with her family, you know," Carrie said. "Everything hasn't been so easy and terrific for her."

"I know," Sam agreed reluctantly, looking over at Emma and Kurt who were being congratulated by a huge crowd of people. "But just once I'd like to know what it feels like to be the poor-little-rich-girl myself!"

"Hey, I've got to be back to baby-sit for the kids in an hour and a half," Carrie said, looking at her watch. "Want to go get something to eat, or are you too full from stuffing yourself all afternoon?"

"*Moi?*" Sam asked. "I'm always up for

14

food. Should we ask the guys or just get Emma?"

"I vote for just Emma," Carrie decided. "The three of us haven't had a chance to talk for days."

"You got it," Sam said. "I'll go get Princess Grace and we'll meet you at the Play Café in a few."

Fifteen minutes later, Emma, Sam and Carrie were comfortably ensconced in their favorite booth under the video monitor in the Play Café. Sam had already ordered a plate of nachos and cheese. All three girls munched while waiting for a deluxe pizza to arrive—of which Sam had already announced she intended to eat at least half.

"Not that you can't have a piece, Emma," Sam said, between bites of nachos, "but I understand when you're totally in love you don't have much of an appetite. Right, Carrie?"

Carrie barely smiled. "I wouldn't know," she said quietly. "Right now I don't think I know much about love."

"What do you mean?" Emma asked her, taking a sip of water. "Billy is crazy about you! Everyone can see that."

15

"It's not Billy." Carrie sighed. "It's Josh."

"Josh again?" Emma asked with surprise. "I thought you already dealt with that!"

"Well, so did I, sort of," Carrie replied.

Josh was Carrie's old high school boyfriend, with whom she'd had a long-term relationship.

"So what's the problem?" Sam asked, reaching for another nacho. "He's there; Billy's here. Love the one you're with, that's what I always say."

Patsi, a waitress who had worked at the Play Café for two summers in a row, placed a large deluxe pizza in front of them. Sam and Emma each took a piece, but Carrie just played with the straw in her diet Coke.

"The problem, guys," Carrie said slowly, "is that I got a letter from New Jersey today, from Josh. And he told me that he's started going out with someone else. And that it could get serious."

"No wonder you dropped that water balloon today," Sam joked. "You were thinking about Josh while you were playing catch with Billy."

"I just don't know what to think any-

16

more," Carrie said. "I mean, I thought that this might happen, and I told myself that this is a free country, and that Josh is free to do exactly what I'm doing. But now that it's actually happening, I feel awful!"

"Well, he was your first love," Emma said. "It must be hard to let go."

Carrie nodded miserably. "I know how unfair I'm being; I just can't help myself!"

"Hey, you're being way too hard on yourself, if you want my opinion," Sam said, licking some cheese off her finger.

"I just feel so . . . torn!" Carrie said earnestly. She looked over at Emma who was daintily biting into a slice of pizza. "You're so lucky," she told her.

"No kidding she's lucky," Sam piped up. "All the money in the world and the most buff guy on the island. I say share the wealth!"

"No, I'm serious, Sam," Carrie said. "When I look at Kurt and Emma together, laughing, joking, just hanging out, I know that they are the only ones for each other in the entire world. I feel . . . well, I just want the same thing for myself."

Emma nodded. "I know. I'm really lucky. But isn't it impossible to love two guys at the same time? I mean, I could never love some other guy as much as I love Kurt, not unless Kurt and I weren't together anymore, and I don't believe that will happen."

"It won't," Carrie said with a sigh. "Sometimes I agree with Sam—you really do seem to lead a charmed life!"

"Oh, I don't . . ." Emma protested.

"I'm just kidding," Carrie said. "Sort of."

"Hey, not to interrupt the heavy sighing going on here, but do either of you want the last slice of pizza?" Sam asked.

"We could never deprive you," Carrie told her.

"Good," Sam said happily, reaching for the slice. "Then I'll give you some of my best advice-to-the-lovelorn. You know I think much better on a full stomach!"

"Speak, oh wise-one," Carrie told her.

"Okay, here's the deal," Sam said, happily chomping on the pizza. "Billy is crazed for you and you are crazed for him. Josh is still pining away for you, but your feelings for him are based more on what was than what is. Have I got that right?"

"Sort of," Carrie said, "But I do still love Josh. . . ."

"Well, that's different," Sam said. "In

that case, I recommend stringing Josh along for some time to come."

"That's terrible advice!" Emma exclaimed.

"And completely unfair!" Carrie added.

"Yeah, but it's probably what you'll do, anyway," Sam said philosophically.

Carrie didn't say anything. She was too afraid that Sam was right.

TWO

"It's a perfect Zit People song," Ian Templeton said emphatically.

"Is not," retorted Allie Jacobs.

"Is too!"

"Is not!"

"Is!"

"Uh, maybe you guys should just try it out and see how it actually plays?" Carrie ventured equivocally, from the top step of the Templeton's basement.

It was the next day and she and Sam were watching fourteen-year-old Ian's band, Lord Whitehead and the Zit People, at one of their biweekly rehearsals. Since Allie and Becky Jacobs, the fourteen-year-old identical twins that Sam took care of, had recently been added to the band as backup singers, Sam had come over with them to watch the rehearsal. The other four members of the Zit People stood around looking bored during this exchange between Ian and Allie.

"Sometimes I wonder if the band would put up with Ian if he wasn't Graham Perry's son," Sam whispered to Carrie.

Ian's dad, Graham Templeton—or as he was known to the public, Graham Perry—was one of the top rock stars in the world.

"Sometimes I wonder the same thing," Carrie agreed with a sigh. "What really gets me is that Ian is such a great kid when he's not working on this band thing!"

"Well, you'd never know it to watch him right now," Sam observed.

"I can handle this myself, Carrie," Ian said, an exasperated look on his face.

Carrie traded looks with Sam. "I guess having his baby-sitter butt in is not high on Ian's hit parade," Sam murmured.

"Look," Ian said, turning to his band, "What kind of music does this band—*my* band—play?"

"Industrial music!" piped up Mark Woods, one of the original members of the band.

"Whether we have backup singers or not!" Becky and Allie Jacobs both shot him spiteful looks.

"And what is industrial music?" he asked them.

"Atonal music for the post–industrial age," Donald Zuckerman singsonged, rolling his eyes heavenward.

"That's right," Ian approved. "You can't think of these hulked-out appliances we play as appliances or you miss the whole point!"

"What *is* the point?" Becky demanded, her hands on her hips. "I hope you figure it out before I reach middle age."

"Let me review," Ian said, ignoring Becky and folding his arms superciliously. The entire group groaned. "Who formed this band, brought you all into it, picked the music, and then led this band to its first success, the gig at Cleve Parker's party?" Ian asked.

"You did," the whole band chanted, sounding bored to death.

Sam recalled that the Zit People had played at a birthday party for a thirteen-year-old kid earlier in the summer, and that they actually sounded almost okay on one song, an industrialized version of "Motherless Child."

"Then for the moment, and for the foreseeable future," Ian said, "I continue to be the Sultan of Selection. That is, I choose the tunes."

"Your dad's going to lose it," Becky warned.

"Yeah," Allie agreed. "When he hears 'I Run for Cover' done the Zit People way, we are history."

"We wouldn't want to tick off your dad," Mark Woods said nervously, biting at a hangnail.

Ian's face got bright red. "Look, if you guys are in this band just because of my dad, then you should get out right now. Well?"

"No . . . uh, it's cool," Donald assured him nervously. "You know your dad better than we do, I guess."

"Am I getting this right?" Sam whispered to Carrie. "The Zits here are planning to cover Graham's number one hit?"

"Looks like it," Carrie winced. "God, I hope Graham doesn't have a fit."

"Well, I'd have a fit if I heard my biggest hit played on a broken-down washing machine and a Cuisinart!" Sam exclaimed.

"Okay everyone, we're about to make 'I Run for Cover' ours!" Ian declared, standing in front of the cassette player. "We're doing it the Zit People way! Places, everyone!"

Sam and Carrie watched as Allie and Becky slunk back to their spots at the backup singers' microphone, and each boy took his place behind a hulked-out appliance.

"Okay, one . . . two . . . one, two, three, four—" Ian counted off and then flipped the switch on the tape deck. Then he ran to take his place in front of the microphone. The opening strains of his father's smash hit filled the room:

"I run for cover
Under cover of darkness
You shine your lovelight
In a spotlight so heartless"

Within seconds, Graham's gorgeous rock baritone was completely drowned out by

25

the sound of metal pipes banging on a microwave oven, a Cuisinart, a washing machine and a Mr. Coffee, and by Allie and Becky Jacobs repeating the words "Under cover, under cover, under cover," again and again.

"Uh, let's make our escape!" Carrie yelled into Sam's ear. Sam nodded emphatically, and the two girls slipped out of the basement while the song was still playing.

They ran into the Templeton's den, Sam shaking her head and laughing hysterically. The sounds of the Zit People could still be faintly heard, but the Templeton's basement was pretty much soundproof. *Thank God,* Sam thought.

"They've got a ways to go, don't you think?" Carrie asked, as she and Sam settled down on the Templeton's couch and Sam flipped on MTV. As fate would have it, the music video of the original "I Run for Cover" was just beginning. Sam and Carrie laughed until their sides hurt.

"Uh, yeah," Sam replied, when the song was over, still shaking her head back and forth. "They've got a ways to go. And at the rate they're going, they'll never get there!" Both girls cracked up again.

"Listen, I hate to break into this levity, but what did you decide about Josh and Billy?" Sam asked, becoming serious. She reached for some candy in a dish on the coffee table.

"I've basically made a decision about it," Carrie told Sam.

"So?" Sam asked, raising her eyebrows.

"It's over with Josh," Carrie said, sighing, "so I'm going to make it really over."

"No way!" Sam exclaimed.

"Yep," Carrie said, staring at the television with a faraway look in her eyes. "I'm going to write to Josh, wish him the very best and tell him that I hope we can stay friends in the future."

"You told him that before but you couldn't stick to it," Sam reminded her friend.

"Well, this time I'm determined," Carrie declared. "I'm sticking to it."

"Whoa, baby!" Sam exclaimed. "A real life Dear John letter! Lemme read it before you actually send it. Then again, don't bother. That's one kind of letter I'll *never* be sending. Two guys for every girl are odds I can live with."

Carrie smiled grimly. "I've got to do what's fair. It's not going to be easy, but I'm going to do it anyway."

"Hope it's not a letter you're going to regret," Sam said lightly.

"I'll never know till I do it, will I?" Carrie asked.

All Sam could do was nod in reply.

Three hours later, rehearsal over, Sam and the twins returned to the Jacobses' house. It was midafternoon, and the mail had arrived, per usual, around one o'clock. While the twins went into the kitchen to fix themselves a snack, Sam flipped through the stack of correspondence. There were the usual bills for Dan Jacobs, the twins' father, a sweepstakes announcement, a copy of *Newsweek* magazine, and at the bottom of the pile, a letter addressed to Sam with a return address in Oakland, California.

A letter from my birth mother, Sam thought to herself, and as usual when she saw the now-familiar return address, she had mixed emotions.

It had been devastating to find out at the age of nineteen, purely by chance, that she

28

was adopted. Adopted! And her parents had never told her! It was the biggest shock of her life. For a while she'd been so angry with her parents that she'd barely spoken with them. How could she possibly trust them after such a major betrayal?

Sam decided to search for her birth mother, and through an organization called the Adoption Finders Agency, Sam had discovered that at the very same time her birth mother was searching for her!

As Sam stared at Susan's letter, she recalled how her birth mother had flown to Sunset Island from her home in Oakland, California to meet Sam. Sam had fantasized that her birth mother would be tall, gorgeous and glamorous, but Susan had turned out to be short and only moderately attractive—in a quiet sort of way.

During Susan's visit, Sam got the second biggest shock of her life—Susan told her the story of how and why she'd given Sam up for adoption.

She explained to Sam that she'd already been married at the time, and had been told she could never conceive a child, so she and her husband, Carson, had adopted a baby. A few years later, Susan's marriage was breaking up and she went to Israel to be alone and to think. There she met and fell in love with an Israeli soldier named Michael Blady.

When she returned to California with the intention of ending her marriage, she found out her son, Adam, was gravely ill. She also found out that she could get pregnant, because she was. Somehow while Susan and Carson kept up their vigil at Adam's bedside, they put their marriage back together. When Carson found out Susan was pregnant by another man, he insisted that Susan have an abortion or give the child up for adoption. If she refused, their marriage would be over.

Susan chose to have the child and put it up for adoption. Sam had bitterly asked Susan why she bothered to give birth to her at all, and Susan explained that she always prayed that one day she would find Sam and get to know her, and now her prayers had come true.

It was all too much—it made Sam's head reel. Not only did she have a birth mother who was a children's book editor, she had

an older brother who had recently gradu-
ated from UCLA and a baby sister named
Sarah. On top of that, her birth father was
Israeli and she was Jewish! Jewish! Sam
didn't even know that many Jewish people,
and she knew absolutely nothing about the
faith, except that she was pretty sure they
didn't celebrate Christmas.

Since Susan's visit Sam and Susan had
written back and forth a few times. The
letters were always breezy and friendly,
but still Sam felt torn—almost disloyal—to
her parents whenever she read one. *Well,
now is as good a time as any,* she told
herself, and quickly tore open the envelope.

Dear Sam,

I have been giving this a lot of
thought. I've really been enjoying our
letter-writing, but I have to admit,
something is missing. I'm here and
you're there, and words on paper can't
compare with our actually being together. I can't describe for you the
feeling that I got when I actually came
to Sunset Island and met you. It was

the happiest day of my life and also the scariest. It was like I finally opened and walked through a door that I knew was there for so much of my life, and you were on the other side. But I also knew how hard it was for you.

I know I mentioned that I hoped one day you would come and visit me here in California. I am hoping that that day has arrived. I want to invite you to California this up-coming weekend (perhaps a long weekend?) to visit with Carson, Sarah, and me. Adam, your brother, will be in from UCLA and you can meet him, too. Don't worry about the ticket. We have frequent flier miles and I'll just cash them in. If we are really going to get to know each other it is going to take a big effort. I am willing to make that effort. Please call and say yes. I send you nineteen years of love.

Susan

"Bye, Sam. We're going shopping with Kelly," Allie said as she raced by Sam.

"With what money?" Sam asked absently, still staring at the letter from Susan.

"Dad gave us guilt bucks," she said.

"Uh-huh," Sam said, still staring at the letter. It wasn't until after the door slammed and she heard a car pulling out of the driveway that she realized she didn't know who Kelly was and she didn't know what Allie meant by "guilt bucks." Well, it was too late now. She'd have to grill the twins later. *I just hope whoever Kelly is she's actually old enough to drive legally,* Sam thought as she made her way up to her room.

She fell onto her bed and stared at the ceiling.

Great, just great, she thought. *Carrie thinks she has problems because she has two boyfriends. How would she feel if she had two mothers?*

Now Susan wants to fly me to California to meet the family! This is all happening too fast. Please, why can't I just have problems like Carrie? Nice, normal, teenage problems? Who can I talk to about this?

Sam immediately knew the answer to her own question: Pres. Shortly after Sam had found out that she was adopted, Pres had told her that he was adopted, too. He

was the only one who could possibly understand what she was feeling. Sam reached
for her phone and dialed his number.

"Hello?" he answered, in his easy Tennessee drawl.

"Pres, it's me," Sam said, her voice
cracking with emotion. "You're not going to
believe what just happened." Sam read
him Susan's letter over the phone.

Pres whistled when Sam was finished.
"That's serious business," he said gently.

"I know," Sam replied.

"So, how do you feel about it?" Pres
asked.

"I don't know." Sam admitted. "I'm totally confused!"

"What say I come over and pick you up,
and we go for a ride and talk about it?"

"Would you?" Sam asked eagerly. "I've
only got a couple of hours before I have to
make dinner for the monsters," Sam replied, "but if we could just talk for a
while . . ."

"You got it," Pres agreed easily. "I'll be
over in ten minutes."

Fifteen minutes later, Pres and Sam
were barrelling along Shore Road on Pres's

motorcycle, with Sam gratefully resting her helmeted head on Pres's shoulders, her arms around his muscled stomach. *This feels wonderful,* she thought. *Nice, simple, perfect. Why can't everything be like this?*

Pres slowed down and pulled into a small parking lot by the far pier at the north end of the island. He stopped the bike, and Sam and he attached their helmets to the back. Then they walked, hand-in-hand and in silence, out to the end of the pier. They passed some fishermen and crabbers in the late afternoon sunshine. At the end of the pier, though, they were alone. They sat down on a bench and watched the sun drop slowly in the sky. They could barely make out the glint of light on some of the buildings in Portland. Sam snuggled up against Pres, who held her close.

Pres spoke first. "Have you decided if you want to go out to California?" he asked her gently.

Sam shook her head no, and stared out at the water.

"You know, you're lucky," he told her. "I've been trying to find my biological mother for a long time and I haven't had a bit of luck. You found yours real quick."

"I know," Sam said in a low voice.

"You're also lucky that she wants to know you and have you be a part of her life," Pres said quietly. "It could have worked out a lot differently."

"It's just that everything's happening so fast, Pres," Sam said, as Pres nuzzled his face in her neck.

"Sometimes life's like that. And sometimes things just take forever," Pres said. "Dang if I can figure it out."

"So you're saying that I should go?" Sam asked in a troubled voice.

"You're the only one can decide that," Pres said.

"I'm asking for your opinion," Sam persisted.

"Okay then, my opinion is that you should go if you're ready to go," Pres replied.

"And I have to figure out if I'm ready," Sam said with a sigh.

Pres nodded.

"What if I can't?" Sam asked.

"No such thing as can't, girl," Pres said. "Won't, maybe, but not can't."

Sam stared and him and grinned. "You sure are philosophical for a country boy," she teased.

"We might talk real slow, but we think real fast," Pres said, and leaned over to give Sam a sweet, tender kiss.

Sam kissed him back, and wished her life could be as easy and sweet as those kisses.

Pres dropped Sam back at the Jacobses' house just in time for her to make dinner for the twins. As she boiled water for noodles and made a salad, she thought about her conversation with Pres. *Even if I did want to go to California there's no guarantee that Mr. Jacobs would give me the time off,* Sam thought to herself. *Yeah, well, first you have to figure out if you want to go at all,* a voice in her head insisted.

While Becky and Allie were gobbling up their macaroni and cheese (they were on one of their eat-everything-in-sight kicks instead of their diet-until-you-die-of-malnutrition kicks), Dan Jacobs walked in, carrying several full shopping bags from the Sunset Sports Shop on Main Street.

"Hi, girls. Hi, Sam!" Dan sang out, as he walked into the kitchen. Sam greeted him warmly, and the twins mumbled a bored hello. Dan was smiling broadly.

"You'll never guess what's in these bags," he said to the twins, motioning to the shopping bags on the floor.

"Falsies for Sam?" Becky guessed sweetly. Allie snorted a laugh and Sam shot them both killer looks.

"It's for you guys," Dan told his daughters, totally ignoring their rudeness, Sam noted.

The twins immediately bolted from the table and started tearing through the bags.

Sam saw all sorts of things fly out. Insect repellent. Fishing equipment. Mosquito netting. A two-person tent. Two wool shirts. A tiny propane stove. Flashlights.

"Excuse me?" Allie asked her father. "Did you get us mixed up with someone else's daughters?"

"Someone with no fashion sense, maybe?" Becky added, gingerly holding up a gray wool shirt.

Dan laughed. "No one worries about fashion on a camping trip," he laughed, picking up one of the flashlights and shining it against the wall of the kitchen. "We're going camping this weekend."

"Correction, Dad," Becky said, starting to edge her way out of the kitchen. "You are going camping. I am staying here on the island."

"Ditto," Allie agreed. "My idea of roughing it is a hotel without room service."

"It's going to be great," Dan said enthusiastically. "I've already made reservations for us at Sebago Lake State Park in Raymond. It's not all that far from Portland and it's supposed to be beautiful."

"Count me out, Pops," Becky said, returning to her macaroni. "I'd rather stay here and work on my music."

"And I'd rather stay here and do *anything*," Allie added.

Dan still looked unperturbed. "Well, I suppose you can stay if you really want. But we're going with the Peters kids from Boston," Dan said lightly.

The twins sat up and took notice. "The Peters kids, as in Bill and Chris Peters?" Allie asked excitedly.

"The ones training for the Olympics in gymnastics?" Becky added.

"The totally, awesomely, unbelievably buff Bill and Chris Peters who you said were too old for us?" Allie asked.

"Yeah, but they're not because they're only fifteen and sixteen," Becky said, "and they both think I'm really, really cute?"

"They do not think you're cute," Allie corrected her sister, "and besides, you're not going camping. I am, though, Dad," she added for her father's benefit.

"I'm going, too, you imbecile," Becky snapped, jumping out of her seat. "Lemme try out that flashlight, Dad," she said, reaching for the light. "I'll need it after dark to navigate with Bill and Chris."

Dan Jacobs frowned. "Becky . . ."

"Just kidding, Dad!" she assured him.

"Not," Allie added under her breath.

"It'll be super!" Dan assured his daughters. "I'll just go call Sid and Cheryl Peters and tell them we're all set."

Sam followed him into the den and cleared her throat. "Uh, Mr. Jacobs, I mean Dan?" she asked. She still didn't feel comfortable using his first name, although he had asked her to.

"Yes?" Dan asked.

"Am I, uh, supposed to go on this camping trip?" *Please let him say no,* Sam prayed. *Camping out with the monsters is my idea of purgatory.*

"Well, gee, if you really want to, it's okay," Dan told her. "I mean, I certainly didn't mean to exclude you—"

"Oh, no!" Sam rushed in as quickly as she could. "I don't feel excluded. Not at all!"

"Good," Dan replied. "I think I could really use this trip to bond with my daughters."

"Bond," Sam repeated, nodding seriously. "Good idea. I'm sure it'll be terrific." *Actually, I'm sure it'll be a nightmare,* she thought to herself.

"Thanks," Dan said. "So have a great time, whatever you do."

And then it hit her. She was free. She could go to California if she wanted to. There was nothing standing in her way . . . except maybe herself.

"Listen, I might not spend the weekend here," she heard herself telling Dan before she could even stop and think about what she was doing.

41

"Oh, really?" he asked, looking up the Peters's number in the address book by the phone.

"Yeah," Sam answered. "There's a chance I might go out to California to, uh, visit some family I haven't seen in a while."

"Sure, no problem." Dan said easily. "Just be back by Tuesday morning, which is when we'll be back."

Sam agreed and ran upstairs to her room. "I guess you've made a decision, after all," she told her reflection in the mirror. She waited a few minutes for Dan to get off the phone. Then she looked up and dialed Susan Briarly's number in California.

"Hello?" a male voice answered.

"Uh, this is Samantha Bridges in Maine. Can I talk to Susan, please?" Sam said, her voice cracking a little.

"Just a minute, please," the voice responded gruffly. Sam heard the phone bang on a table. "Susan!" the voice shouted. "It's for you!" *I still have time to back out,* Sam told herself. *All I have to say is, sorry—*

"Hello, this is Susan," Sam heard her birth mother say into the phone.

"Susan, it's me, Sam," Sam heard herself say. "I got your letter today."

"Yes?" Susan asked, her voice full of hope.

Sam gulped hard and took a deep breath. "I'll see you on Saturday."

THREE

"Carrie! Lookit lookit lookit!" The chirpy voice of three-year-old Chloe Templeton carried over the sounds of the other kids playing in the Sunset Country Club kiddie pool. "Lookit me!"

"I'm lookiting!" Carrie yelled back, a big smile on her face. She was stretched out on a chaise lounge by the side of the pool, and her friends Emma and Sam were right by her side. They were all there baby-sitting for their respective kids and enjoying a typically gorgeous Maine summer morning at the same time. Allie and Becky Jacobs were practicing diving at the deep end of the pool, and the two older kids that Emma took care of, Wills and Ethan Hewitt, were doing surface dives for pennies.

45

"She's a sweet kid," Emma said to Carrie.

"She is," Carrie agreed, "but she's also a handful."

"Katie too," Emma said, and she had to smile just thinking about the energetic little girl. "I love her to death but I'm glad Jane Hewitt decided to take her shopping this morning. Ethan and Wills can usually entertain themselves."

"Unless one of them drowns the other," Sam said, cocking her head towards the two boys, who were screaming at each other at the top of their lungs.

"It doesn't count if you hid the penny in your swim trunks!" Wills screeched at his older brother.

"Don't be such a crybaby!" Ethan snorted back.

"You're the baby!" Wills cried, splashing water at his brother. Ethan responded by dunking a sputtering Wills under the water.

"I spoke too soon," Emma said, quickly going over to the side of the pool. "Hey, guys, cut it out," she admonished them quietly.

"I hate him!" Wills yelled, on the verge of tears.

"Boohoo, boohoo," Ethan taunted his little brother.

"Ethan, come on," Emma chided him. "Don't pick on Wills."

"Okay, I'll leave the baby alone," Ethan said, hoisting himself out of the pool. "I've got better things to do, anyway." He grabbed his towel and headed towards the game room.

"I'll just dive for pennies by myself," Wills mumbled, clearly embarrassed that other kids had seen his brother belittling him.

"Good idea," Emma agreed. "And on the way home we'll stop at Sweet Stuff for ice cream, if you want."

"Okay," Wills agreed shyly, and began diving again for the pennies.

"Another crisis averted," Emma said lightly, returning to her chaise.

"God, remind me not to have any children," Sam said. "What a pain!" She reached into her bag and pulled out some sun block and poured some on her legs.

"That's a great bathing suit," Carrie told Sam.

Sam looked down at her tiny black bikini, held together at the sides with brass rings. "Oh, this old thing," she joked, rubbing the lotion into her legs.

Carrie looked down at her old navy blue maillot and sighed. "How do you always manage to wear new stuff on such a limited budget?"

"I never met a fashion opportunity I didn't seize," Sam said with a shrug. "For example, Allie bought this suit, but when she tried it on at home she fell right out of the top. So I traded her one of my Disney World staff T-shirts for the bathing suit and saved Allie the trouble of returning the suit."

"Amazing," Carried marveled.

"Are you serious about not wanting kids?" Emma asked Sam.

"Totally," Sam told her. "How would you feel about kids if you had to spend not one, but two summers looking after the monsters?" Sam gestured to the Jacob twins down by the diving board. Allie had just done a forward somersault off the high board, and since one of the guys had untied the bottom of her bikini she held it closed and squealed through the entire dive. All the boys around the pool were hooting at her.

"Yo, Allie!" Sam yelled out. "Maybe that's not the best dive you could do!"

"Hey, Sam!" Allie yelled back from in the pool. "Maybe you shouldn't be telling me what to do!"

Sam turned back to her friends. "See what I mean? I'm so glad they're going to be away this weekend. It'll give me a break." Her voice dropped confidentially. "And . . . a chance to go to California."

"You're going *where?*" Carrie asked, her eyes scanning the kiddie pool to make sure Chloe was doing okay.

"California," Sam answered nonchalantly. "It's a country just west of the United States. I understand they speak English there. Weird English, but English."

"But why?" Emma asked.

"And how?" Carrie added.

"Why is because my birth mother wrote

and invited me," Sam told them. "And how is because she's paying for the plane ticket." Sam went on and told them how Susan lived in Oakland—which was just across the bay from San Francisco—and how Dan Jacobs had decided to take the twins camping, which meant she was actually free to go.

"So basically, I'm outta here," Sam said with a flourish, pulling on her leopard-print sunglasses.

"Well, that's great," Emma told Sam, but something about Sam's complete nonchalance nagged at her. "I mean, you feel really good about this, right?"

"Right," Sam agreed, glad her friends couldn't see her eyes. *Why don't I just tell them how ambivalent I feel?* she asked herself. *Why do I always feel like I have to put up some kind of a front?*

"So . . . you're not nervous at all?" Carrie asked.

"No, everything's cool," Sam assured her.

She's not altogether sure about this, Carrie thought to herself. *Well, I've got some interesting news for her. Watch me play this one a la Sam Bridges.*

"Cool, Sam," Carrie said nonchalantly, "Guess I'll meet you under the Golden Gate Bridge on Saturday night."

"Yeah, sure," Sam said, taking the bait. "And on Sunday we'll ride the cable car to Fisherman's Wharf. I know all the cool San Francisco tourist places. See?" She dug into her pocketbook, and pulled out *San Francisco in 48 Hours,* a guidebook she had purchased at the bookstore on Main Street.

Carrie saw her opening. She reached into her denim knapsack and pulled out the same guidebook. She held it up with a dramatic wave.

"Hey, what're you doing with that book!?" Sam cried.

"Just like I said," Carrie smiled, "I'm going to be in San Francisco this weekend. Chloe! Be careful!" Chloe Templeton was practicing putting her head underwater, and kids were splashing all around her in the kiddie pool.

"No way!" Sam fairly screamed with happiness.

"Yep," Carrie said. "Graham is doing this big show at the Oakland Coliseum—

some sort of benefit for the environment with Billy Joel—and he's decided to take the whole family. I'm going along to look after Ian and Chloe."

"Well, poor me," Emma sighed dramatically. "I'm marooned here with only Kurt Ackerman to entertain me."

"Ha," Sam snorted. "Wear that bathing suit you have on and he'll be entertaining you plenty."

"It's his favorite," Emma said dreamily, looking down at her white, halter-necked bathing suit with the high cut legs.

"Too mushy for me," Sam announced. "Someone needs to hose down your mind."

"Look who's talking!" Carrie hooted.

"Seriously," Emma told them, leaning forward on her elbow, "you two will love San Francisco. It's just about my favorite city on earth. The beach, the food, the cable cars, the nightclubs—"

"Nightclubs?" Sam asked, "Did I hear you say nightclubs?"

"In the south of the Market Street area," Emma explained, "there are a lot of new rock clubs."

"I'm there!" Sam announced gleefully. "What do you know about Oakland?"

"I haven't actually been there—it's over near Berkeley," Emma said. "I've heard there are some very nice sections, especially up in the hills."

"Too bad you're not coming with us," Sam told Emma. "You'd be the ultimate guide."

"Sam's right," Carrie agreed. "It would be incredible if you could come, too." She looked over at Chloe, who was being pushed by a bigger girl and looked ready to cry. "Oops, Carrie to the rescue," she called and dashed over to Chloe.

"So?" Sam asked Emma.

"I'd love to—" Emma said.

"That's great!" Sam interrupted with her usual enthusiasm. "We'll turn the town upside down. We'll have a blast! We'll—"

"I'd love to, but I can't," Emma said firmly.

"Why not?" Sam pouted.

Emma pointed to Ethan and Wills, who were now shooting at each other with high-powered water guns in the play area off to the side of the pool. "That's why," she said. "I'm working, remember?"

"That girl doesn't like me," Chloe said

solemnly as Carrie led her over to Sam and Emma.

"Well, we like you," Emma told the little girl. "Sit with us." Chloe got on the chaise lounge with Carrie and snuggled against her au pair.

"Carrie, I'm trying to get Ms. Cresswell here to come to California with us, and she's giving me some lame-o excuse," Sam said.

"What's that?" Carrie asked.

"She claims she's—now get this—working!" Sam said, rolling her eyes.

"Not an acceptable excuse," Carrie teased. "Give her five days detention and make her write 'going to San Francisco is the right thing to do' five thousand times on the blackboard."

"Sorry," Emma said sadly, "I've got to stay here. Look! There's Darcy Laken. I asked her to stop by and hang out with us, and she didn't know if she could."

"Bogus," Sam grunted. "Laken comes through in the clutch, while Cresswell bombs out when the going gets tough."

"Sam!" Emma and Carrie said at the same time. Then they all laughed.

"What's the joke?" Darcy exclaimed,

pulling up a chair by her friends. She was dressed casually, in a pair of high cut-off jeans that showed off her muscular legs and a University of Maine T-shirt.

Carrie told her how she and Sam were both going to be in California this upcoming weekend, and how they were trying to convince Emma to take the time off and come with them. "Of course," she finished, "we could leave Emma here and get you to come with us."

"No dice," Darcy said. "Big-time horror-theme dinner party this weekend at the Mason house, and I've agreed to dress as Lady Dracula and help serve. Hope they don't plan on serving raw lamb chops, but with Molly's parents, you never know!" The girls cracked up.

"Anyway, Emma," Darcy said, "I've got a feeling you should go with Sam and Carrie."

The girls all looked at each other. Darcy had this weird knack of getting ESP flashes at the oddest times, and when she got a feeling about something, it was usually right on target.

If only she could control it, Sam thought

enviously to herself, *she could get her own television series.*

"Is this one of your flashes?" Emma asked, closing her eyes and touching her forehead in imitation of a nightclub psychic.

"Nope, just an opinion," Darcy said easily.

"Well, how about you ring up the spirit world and ask their opinion," Sam said. "Maybe they'll help me convince her."

"Nice try, Sam," Emma laughed, "but I'd feel guilty even asking Jane and Jeff for the time off."

"Do you have to be so perfect all the time?" Sam groaned.

"That's me, walking perfection," Emma said lightly as she got up from the chaise lounge. There had been a time when Sam's teasing had bothered her, but that was in the past. "I have to run," she said, sticking her towel in her beach bag. "I've got to get the kids home for lunch."

"Call me," Carrie called to her.

"Me too," Sam added. "I'm still going to try to talk you into it."

Emma waved good-naturedly to her friends and went to fetch Ethan and Wills.

"That girl is entirely too responsible," Sam groused to Carrie and Darcy.

"Well, I don't know about that," Darcy said, the sun beating down on her face. "But I do think she should go with you guys."

"Couldn't you just tell her you had some kind of psychic flash about it?" Sam pleaded.

"Sorry, psychic flashes aren't something I take lightly," Darcy told Sam. "You'll have to talk Emma into it on your own."

"Well, you know my motto," Sam told them, "never say never!"

"Good luck," Darcy offered sleepily, and turned over to get some sun on the back of her legs.

"You ready to turn in?" Darcy asked Molly. It was about eleven o'clock that night, and Darcy had been in her room reading a book on criminology, a subject that fascinated her.

Molly put her own book down and yawned. "Yeah, I'm sleepy." She snuggled down into her bed.

"I wish you would've come to the club

with me this morning," Darcy told Molly. "It was fun."

"For you, maybe," Molly told her. "I can't stand the thought of going back there during prime time. All those perfect-looking girls with their long, tanned legs staring at me in my wheelchair . . ." she shuddered just thinking about it.

"Well, if you ever change your mind, just let me know," Darcy told her lightly. "Good night."

Darcy went to her room and got ready for bed, but even though she was tired, she tossed and turned for a while. Something was bothering her, something about the club. *It must be Molly,* Darcy thought to herself. *I hope some day she'll say to hell with what anyone thinks and just do what she wants to do—go to the club, go to restaurants, go to California if she wants to!*

"Now, what made me think of California?" she asked herself out loud, but fell asleep before she could answer the question.

She slept fitfully, but snapped awake in the middle of the night. *I was dreaming,* she remembered, *something . . . something important, something about Emma.* Quickly she sat up and turned on the light, then reached for a pen and a piece of paper.

She wrote:

Dreamt Emma In San Fran. Some park? Emma sitting under tree. Very foggy and spooky. Emma had big magic marker. Writing on sheets of newsprint. Writing "This is the right thing to do" a million times.

Darcy stopped. That was all she could remember. What did it mean? She couldn't figure it out. After running it over and over in her mind for nearly an hour, she was no closer to understanding the dream than when she started. Finally, she drifted back to sleep.

When she awoke the next morning, she went downstairs and fixed herself a cup of coffee. None of the Masons were awake yet, so she brought in the *Boston Globe,* which they had delivered every day, read the front section and the sports section, and watched the clock until it reached nine A.M. Then she dialed Emma's number.

"Hewitt residence," Emma answered.

Darcy could hear the clanking sounds of breakfast being served in the background.

"Emma, it's Darcy," Darcy said, feeling a little sheepish for calling.

"Hi! What's up? I can only talk a minute. It's breakfast here," Emma said brightly.

"I had a strange dream about you last night," Darcy said, in her straightforward manner.

"Are you sure Sam didn't put you up to this?" Emma asked with a laugh.

"No, this is legit," Darcy assured her. She read to Emma what she had written down. "I think this means you should go to San Francisco."

Emma was silent a moment. "I think I should go to San Francisco, too," Emma answered finally. "But I can't. So I won't, and that's the end of it. Subject closed."

"I understand how you feel," Darcy said, "but I had to tell you. . . ."

"I guess," Emma agreed. "I've got to run—I'll talk to you soon."

Darcy heard Emma hang up, and then she hung up herself. *Well, I did my best,* Darcy told herself. But she knew that

Emma had made her mind up—she was staying on Sunset Island for the weekend, and no one—not even Darcy—was going to be able to change her mind.

FOUR

Later that day, Emma sat baking in the afternoon sun in the umpire's chair near the tournament-finals tennis court of the Sunset Island Country Club, allegedly watching the cutthroat match between Ethan and his next-door neighbor, Stinky Stein. Her mind kept wandering, though, to what Darcy had told her on the phone. Experience had taught her to trust Darcy's dreams and psychic flashes, but reality said that she just couldn't get away to California for the weekend. *I can't very well tell Jane she has to give me time off because Darcy had a dream about me,* Emma told herself in frustration.

"That ball was clearly in. Right Emma?" Ethan yelled up to her.

Emma's attention snapped back to the

game. "Uh, well . . ." she began tentatively.

"Look!" Ethan said, pointing to a mark in the red clay of the tennis court just near where the service line and the left sideline came together. "There's the mark!"

"Don't call the ball in, Emma, just because little baby Ethan's mother told you that you had to umpire our set because otherwise I might beat him up again and give him another bloody nose! Cry baby!" Stinky said in a rush, kicking at the red court with his tennis shoes.

Emma rolled her eyes. *Umpiring tennis is not one of the things that I'm going to list on my set of career goals,* she thought.

"You're just mad 'cause I'm beating you four to two," Ethan gloated.

"I'm letting you get ahead," Stinky retorted, "so you won't cry like a baby!"

"Shuddup Stinky!" Ethan said. "Was it in or out, Emma?"

You'd never believe these two are best friends off the court, Emma thought to herself. *If they had access to nuclear weapons we'd be about ready for the start of World War III.*

I've got to make up my mind. Well, here

goes nothing. "The umpire refuses to over-rule Mr. Stein's call," Emma said. "The score of this game is thirty-all. Mr. Hewitt continues to lead in the match at four games to two. Mr. Hewitt's serve. Play!" *Hmmmm. Not bad,* Emma smiled to herself. *I sound just like one of the umpires at the US Open. Of course, I could have done it in French, pretended it was the French Open. That would have crossed them up!*

Ethan glared at Emma and stomped back to the baseline to serve. Emma could see that he was really mad. But somehow he managed to channel his anger into his game. Emma watched in amazement as Ethan served two straight aces to win the game and take the lead, five to two. He then blasted back each one of Stinky's serves so that Stinky couldn't even make a return. In five minutes the set was over. *Thank goodness they're only playing one set; I couldn't take another,* Emma thought.

Ethan ran up to the net and jumped over it to shake Stinky's hand.

"Nice match, cry baby," Stinky said, but he reached out his hand to Ethan.

"We'll play again tomorrow," Ethan said. Then, the two boys walked over to Emma, reached up, and each shook her hand as if they had just finished the Wimbledon finals. *Finally,* Emma thought, *I can climb down out of this monkey chair. My back is killing me.*

"C'mon," Emma said to them, as they started to walk back to the main clubhouse, "I'll buy you each a soda."

"Can't, Emma," Stinky said, "My mom said I have to be home by four–thirty. We're going to some concert in Portland tonight. Yuck! I hate all that mushy classical music."

One day, Stinky Stein is going to make some lucky girl really happy. Not! Emma thought, and laughed out loud. "Yeah, me too," Emma joked. She had seen most of the world's great symphony orchestras perform and had been enthralled by many of them. She remembered being dragged to them as a kid, though, and hating it.

"No kidding?" Stinky asked with surprise. "What kind of music do you like?"

"Um . . . industrial music!" Emma said, saying the first thing that popped into her mind.

"Oh yeah, me too!" Stinky agreed enthusiastically. "I heard Lord Whitehead and the Zit People at Cleve's birthday party. They were awesome."

"Totally," Ethan agreed.

Emma stifled a laugh. *Wait until I tell Carrie that The Zits are developing a following!* she thought to herself. *She won't believe it!*

After dropping Stinky off at the Steins's house, Emma and Ethan went home. Emma was actually happy that she didn't have to suffer through a soda with Stinky and Ethan because she had a date for dinner at Rubie's Café with Kurt.

I deserve the break, she thought, walking through the door of the Hewitts. *Up at seven-thirty A.M., swimming lesson for Katie at nine-thirty, baby-sitting at the club until noon, home for lunch with all three kids, then back to the club in the afternoon with Ethan—that's a full day's work!*

Jane was in the kitchen making dinner when Emma came in. Emma had already cleared her date with the Hewitts, so there were only five place settings on the table. Jane had picked some roses from the garden for a centerpiece flower arrangement, and Emma thought the whole thing looked very homey. *Just the way my parents' house never looked,* Emma thought.

"Hi, Emma!" Jane said warmly. "How'd my future tennis champ do?"

"I won!" Ethan said, looking very proud. "And Stinky didn't even hit me this time."

"Well, that's a step in the right direction," Jane agreed, smiling at Emma. "Thanks for umpiring that match, Emma. I think you prevented some major bloodshed." Emma laughed in agreement.

"Go get washed for dinner, Ethan," Jane instructed her son.

"Okay, mom," Ethan answered easily.

Well, well, is he acting nice! He needs to win tennis matches more often, Emma thought.

When Ethan was gone, Jane sat down at the table. "I'm glad we have a few minutes of peace," she said to Emma. "I wanted to talk to you about this upcoming weekend."

"Sure," Emma said, sitting down with Jane.

"Jeff and I decided this morning that we want to go to a legal conference in New York this weekend about Alternative Dispute Resolution," Jane explained. "It's not really my idea of a good time, but we need the continuing legal education credits for the bar, and anyway the subject is interesting."

I barely understand what she's talking about! Emma thought. She nodded as Jane pressed on.

"So anyway, we reserved three hotel rooms at the Grand Hyatt for Friday, Saturday, and Sunday nights, because we were planning to take the kids and you," Jane explained. "But then Jeff pointed out that there was day-care for Katie and that the organizers had planned activities for the other kids."

Emma nodded again. Her heart started to beat faster in her chest. Was Jane getting at what she thought Jane was getting at? Was she really about to get sprung for the weekend?

"So," Jane concluded, "the bottom line is, you're welcome to come with us, although I don't think there's going to be much for you to do. Otherwise, you can have the weekend off—until Tuesday morning."

Thank you, God, fate, or whatever just threw this little opportunity into my lap! Emma exulted to herself. But she had to be sure Jane wasn't just being nice. "Are you sure, Jane?" Emma asked. "Because I'd be happy to go with you if you want."

"It's entirely up to you," Jane assured her, getting up to make a salad. "I'm sure you can find a ton of fun things to do if you stay here."

"You're really sure it's okay?"

"Sure I'm sure," Jane confirmed, cutting tomatoes into the wooden salad bowl.

"Well, what I think I'm going to do then," Emma began slowly, "is . . . go to California!"

"California?" Jane repeated incredulously. "For the weekend?"

Emma nodded eagerly. "Sam's going out to California—to Oakland—to visit . . . some relatives," she said, careful not to mention exactly who the relatives were without checking with Sam first. "And just by the greatest coincidence, Carrie's going to San Francisco to take care of Graham Perry's kids—he's doing some big benefit with Billy Joel, but the whole family is going—and they both asked me to come, but I said I had to work, and—"

"And now you don't," Jane concluded. "I'd call it great timing! Have a blast!"

"You're sure?" Emma asked, still a bit

uncertain. "Because you know if need me, I'll go with you—"

"Emma, stop being so perfect!" Jane chided with a laugh.

"Funny, that's just what Sam told me," Emma said ruefully.

"Honestly, I appreciate your professionalism, you know that," Jane said gently. "But it's really fine for you to go. Live it up! Just be back by Tuesday morning."

"This is fabulous!" Emma exclaimed, jumping up from the table. "Do you mind if I go call Sam and Carrie?"

"Go for it," Jane said, slipping a slice of tomato in her mouth. "And have fun with Kurt tonight," she added, winking at Emma.

She is the greatest employer in the history of employers, Emma thought, as she practically flew up the stairs to her room to call her friends and to get ready for her date with Kurt. *California here we come!*

Three hours later, Emma sat across from Kurt Ackerman at an outdoor table that had been set up just for the two of them at Rubie's Café, a seafood restaurant down by the docks. Rubie's was owned and run by Rubie O'Malley who was like an aunt to

Kurt. She always made a big fuss over Kurt when he came in. Now that Kurt and Emma were a couple, she made a big fuss over Emma, too.

"I can't believe your aunt set an outdoor table for us!" Emma exclaimed, biting enthusiastically into a piece of Rubie's special Key lime pie. "It's so gorgeous out here."

"It sure is," Kurt agreed, taking a bite of the butter pecan ice cream Rubie had brought him for dessert. "And I'm glad that there aren't a million tourists around to spoil the view."

Then the two of them were silent for a few moments, taking in the sound of the waves gently lapping at the docks, the smell of the salt air, the slight metal-on-metal clinking of a sailboat halyard against its mast, the putt-putt of a lone lobster boat coming into harbor for the night.

It's beautiful here, but it's not nearly as gorgeous as this guy sitting across from me, Emma thought to herself happily. She gazed at handsome Kurt, who had on a crew neck black sweater and a pair of faded Levis. But somehow his simple ensemble accentuated his muscular build and natural good looks. Emma herself had dressed in white ballet-style flats, a blue soft cotton miniskirt and a white silk camisole. Over that she wore a demin jacket with patches of lace and ribbons appliquéd here and there.

"Did I mention how terrific you look?" Kurt murmured.

"Hmmmmm, let me think," Emma teased. "I believe you mentioned it once or twice." She stared out at the setting sun and the gulls making lazy circles through the sky. "What a view," she whispered, supremely content.

"I like the view across the table from me, myself," Kurt said, smiling and looking into Emma's eyes.

Emma smiled back at him. "The feeling's mutual." She took his hand gently, loving the feel of his flesh touching hers. "You really don't mind that I'm going out to California this weekend with Carrie and Sam, instead of staying here?"

On their way to the restaurant, Emma had told Kurt, after swearing him to secrecy, about how Sam was going to Oakland to visit her birth mother, and about how she had decided to go out there with her.

Kurt squeezed Emma's hand in return. "No problem," Kurt said easily. "That's my girl, the world traveler."

"Well, I don't travel that much," Emma demurred.

"No?" Kurt asked. "It seems like you just got back from Paradise Island."

"Well, I won that trip," Emma reminded him. "I would have taken you with me if you could have gotten out of work."

"Look, it's cool," Kurt assured her. "I'd be lying if I didn't admit I'm a little jealous. Hey, I'd like to see San Francisco too!"

"I hope we can go there together some day," Emma told him.

"Me too," Kurt agreed. "But that time doesn't seem to be now. Look, Sam's your good friend, and right now she needs your support."

"Thanks," Emma said, smiling at the wonderful guy she loved. "It means a lot to me that you think it's the right thing to do."

"Just don't fall in love with some California muscleman!" Kurt laughed. But Emma could see a worried look somewhere in the back of his eyes.

"So long as Kurt Ackerman's walking

around on this planet, there's no chance that's going to happen," Emma assured him.

"Good," Kurt said, reaching for the check. "Don't worry about this. I painted Rubie's toolshed the other day, so dinner's on her. Now, let's go for a drive. I have a surprise for you out in my car."

"I can't wait," Emma said, kissing him lightly on the cheek. "Let's go." They walked out to Kurt's beat-up old jalopy, but when Emma climbed in, Kurt just started the car and began driving towards the bay side of the island.

"Everything seems pretty normal to me, Mr. Swim Instructor," Emma said, snuggling up against Kurt's side. "What's the big surprise?"

"Just wait," Kurt grinned. "We're almost there."

"Where?" Emma asked. She could smell a faint cologne on Kurt's body. *Nice,* she thought.

"Here," Kurt answered, and he turned the car off the paved road into a small dirt parking lot. He hopped out of the car, ran around to Emma's side, opened Emma's door and helped her out. Then, he ran back to the rear of the car, opened the trunk, and took a large battery-operated tape deck and a flashlight out of the trunk.

"Welcome to the Ackerman nightclub," he joked. Emma cracked up. "Follow me!" Kurt started walking down a narrow vine-entangled path. Emma had no choice but to follow as Kurt lit the way with his flashlight. In just a few moments, the path opened up into a large, sandy clearing. Emma could hear the sound of waves breaking from over a set of dunes.

"Nice nightclub," Emma murmured.

"The best clientele in the world," Kurt said, taking Emma in his arms.

"Mmmmm," Emma murmured in return, basking in the warmth of Kurt's strong arms.

"Shall we dance?" Kurt asked, flipping on the cassette player. The opening notes of Travis Tritt's romantic "Drift Off to Dream" filled the night air. Emma felt herself melt in Kurt's arms, and they danced together in the moonlight. When the song ended, Kurt kissed her slowly until the heat spread from her face to the tips of her toes.

"Wow," Emma said breathlessly. "You make me feel so . . . so . . ."

"Mutual," Kurt murmured into Emma's hair. "I love you so much, Em. I don't want it ever to end."

"It never will," Emma promised passionately, holding him even closer.

"No, I mean it," Kurt said, holding her away from him a moment so that he could stare into her eyes. "You and I should go on forever. You're the best thing that ever happened to me."

"Is that a proposal?" Emma joked.

"No, but maybe it's a proposal for a proposal," Kurt responded seriously.

"I'm . . . not sure what that means," Emma said nervously.

"It means I love you," Kurt said in a husky voice.

"I love you, too," she said simply.

"So then," Kurt asked. "What do you think?"

"About what?"

"About my proposal for a proposal?" Kurt grinned, but Emma saw the same little glint of nervousness in his eyes that she saw at Rubie's Café.

"I propose that you kiss me again," she said, dodging the subject a little.

This time he kissed her harder, as if the force of his lips on hers could guarantee her response to his question. "You know no guy you could meet in any of your travels could be better than this," Kurt said.

"Of course I know that," Emma agreed. "Don't worry, Kurt. I'm not planning to meet any guys in California or anywhere else!"

"Long-distance love doesn't work," Kurt told her. "I've seen great couples torn apart trying to do it."

Emma pulled back and looked into Kurt's eyes. "We're not talking about long-distance love!" she said, a touch of irritation in her voice. "We're talking about one weekend in California!"

"I know," Kurt agreed, running his fingers through her hair. "But I'm not just talking about California. I've given this a lot of thought and I really want you to think about what I said."

"About being . . . engaged to be engaged?" Emma asked him. "Is that really what you want?"

"Of course I do," Kurt said. "Don't you?"

Did she? As Kurt leaned down to kiss her, Emma had two different thoughts—one that she liked, one that scared her to death. *This guy loves me more than anyone could ever love me—and I want to be with him forever*, was the one she liked. *Emma, he's only saying this because he's afraid you're going to meet someone else, because you told him you were going to California*, was the other. And no matter how much Emma tried to banish that particular thought from her mind, it kept on coming back.

FIVE

It was early Saturday morning, and Sam's seat belt was securely fastened when the American Airlines jet took off from Boston's Logan Airport and headed for San Francisco International Airport (or SFX, which is what Emma said sophisticated travelers called it).

Sam's nose was pressed against the glass as the plane made its ascent. *I can't believe that this is the second time this summer that I'm jetting off for some huge trip,* she thought happily to herself. *But I've got to admit I'm nervous about seeing Susan and meeting the rest of my family there. Correction. I don't have to admit it. So I won't!*

The airplane climbed rapidly out of Logan, headed south towards Cape Cod, and then eased into a right turn and began to head west.

"Ladies and gentleman, this is your captain speaking." Sam, and Emma, who was sitting right beside her, heard a male voice announce over the PA system. "Welcome aboard American Flight 33, nonstop from Boston to San Francisco. We'll be cruising at 35,000 feet. There's smooth sailing ahead, so sit back, enjoy the flight, and we'll be in San Francisco in about five hours. Weather at SFX—sixty-one degrees and partly cloudy. If there's anything we can do to make your flight more comfortable, just let one of the flight attendants know."

Soon, an incessant chant came up from a few rows behind Sam and Emma. "We want beer! We want beer! We want beer!" Sam and Emma snapped their heads around to see who was making the racket. They could see that a group of middle-aged men—it looked to Sam like fifteen or more of them—were chanting for beer. And they weren't stopping.

"This is why I always fly first class," Emma said with a sigh.

"Well, excuse me Madam Moneybags,"

Sam said. "Only we low-lifes travel back here in steerage."

"Oh, I didn't mean it like that, Sam," Emma said, lightly touching Sam's arm. "You know I didn't."

"How much more is first class, anyway?" asked Sam, who had never flown first class in her life.

"A lot more," Emma admitted. "But you don't have the Neanderthal chorus in first class. They must be going to some convention."

"We want beer! We want beer!" the men continued chanting.

"Well, thanks for sitting back here with me," Sam said, trying in vain to find a comfortable position for her long legs. "I know you could easily have afforded to be up there with Carrie and the Templetons."

"It's much more fun to sit with you," Emma said easily.

"These seats are made for midgets," Sam groaned. "My legs are bumping into my chin."

"Try sticking them in the aisle to stretch them out," Emma suggested.

Sam turned in her seat and stretched her legs out. "Too bad Graham's private jet is in for an overhaul," Sam said. "Maybe he would have taken all three of us in style!"

"Yo, baby, love them legs!" a male voice hooted.

Sam leaned into the aisle to see who was addressing her.

"Well, aren't you the fox!" the man leered. "Your face is as cute as your legs, baby!"

Sam pulled her face and her legs back in to her seat. "That man is sub-human," she told Emma.

"More beer! More beer! More beer!" the men chanted even more loudly.

"Why doesn't one of the flight attendants tell them to shut up?" Sam asked irritably.

"One of them did," Emma said. "I saw her. They just didn't listen."

"Oh yeah?" Sam asked. With that, she turned around and bellowed, "Yo! You Budweisers back there! Shut up!"

Emma scrunched down in her seat. "Now you've done it, Sam," Emma said, blushing a bright red.

"That's right, I shut them up—"

"Hey! Big Red! This flight'd pass a lot quicker if you'd come sit on—er, by me!" one of them yelled out. His travelmates guffawed heartily.

"Oh great, just great," Emma murmured, sinking even lower in her seat.

"Come on back here and get friendly!" another voice called.

"I'd rather eat road kill!" Sam yelled back, which brought on more hoots and laughter. Some of the other passengers giggled too.

"Sam, you are making a scene!" Emma protested in an icy voice.

Sam raised her eyebrows at Emma. "Hey, you sound just like your mother!"

"Well, this once my mother would be right," Emma muttered.

"I'll fix them," Sam said. "I'm not going to take that kind of abuse. Watch this." Sam reached up and pressed the overhead call button, summoning a flight attendant. A young woman in an American Airlines uniform wearing a name tag that read "Stacey" walked over.

"Stacey, sugar," Sam began, doing an impressive imitation of Lorell Courtland's southern drawl, "would ya'll mind tellin' those boys back there that my father was just hired from Atlanta to be the chief of the San Francisco po-lice, that's he's meetin' me at the airport, and that he'll just be

85

so pleased to hear about how these fine gentlemen have been treatin' his daughter who he hasn't seen in such a long time."

Stacey's head nodded attentively. She'd heard what the one obnoxious man had said to Sam.

"Oh Stacey," Sam added, still in her drawl, "please don't forget to say how the last time Daddy was displeased with one of my boyfriends, that boyfriend passed both Christmas and Groundhog's Day in Emory University Hospital. Thanks, Stacey."

Emma waited until Stacey made her way back to the chanting men before she exploded into laughter. "That was priceless," she exclaimed to Sam. "Wait'll I tell Carrie!"

"I have my moments," Sam replied, turning her head around so she could see Stacey repeating to them what she'd just told her to say. There were a few sarcastic comments full of bravado, but then it got very quiet in the rear of the plane.

"Score redhead one, Budweiser's nothing," Sam said with a laugh, punching the air in victory.

"You are one of a kind, Sam," Emma

said, shaking her head. "Let's go tell Carrie about your exploits."

"Is it okay," Sam asked, "if she's in first class?"

"If she invites us, it's fine," Emma assured her.

The two of them squeezed their way out of their seats, and headed to the first class area where Carrie was napping in a luxurious seat.

"Hey girlfriend, wanna trade places?" Sam asked, nudging Carrie out of her sleep. Carrie opened her eyes, yawned, and stretched.

"Ah, this is the way to travel!" Carrie said.

No kidding, Sam thought. *I'm not meant to get up at six A.M., catch an early plane from Portland to Boston, and then change planes for San Francisco, and sit in coach. It interferes with my beauty rest!*

"Graham and those guys are asleep," Carrie continued, pointing to the front row of seats in the first class section.

"That makes your life easy," Sam whispered, taking a seat next to Carrie.

Carrie stretched and yawned. "I was just having the most delicious dream. . . ."

"About Billy?" Emma asked.

"Actually, in my dream Billy and Josh were both giving me a massage—"

"Well, get down, Carrie!" Sam hooted. "Kinky dream!"

"I've just got Josh on my mind right now," Carrie admitted. "I did what I said I was going to do."

"You wrote to him?" Sam asked.

Carrie nodded. "I did, and I told him it was over."

Sam wiggled her eyebrows comically. "Does that mean he's available?"

"Sam!" Emma protested.

"Just kidding, just kidding," Sam replied breezily.

"So where are you staying in San Francisco?" Emma asked Carrie, trying to change the subject. "We've barely had a chance to make any plans since we decided to go."

"I think the Mark Hopkins on California Street," Carrie replied. "Graham's road manager made the reservations."

"You're kidding!" Emma said, leaning over to rub out a knot in her calf. "We're there, too. Sam and I are sharing a suite. It's a really famous hotel. The cable car line goes right past it."

"You're not staying with Susan?" Carrie asked, looking at Sam.

Sam shrugged. "She invited me, but it just felt too . . . I don't know. . . ."

"Intimate?" Emma suggested.

Sam nodded. "I hardly know her, really."

"Won't she be disappointed?" Carrie asked, "I mean, she's paying for you to come out and everything."

Sam shrugged. "For once I was honest. I told her that I was bringing my friend Emma out for support and that I'd feel better if I stayed in a hotel. She said she understood. Anyway," she added conspiratorially, "it'll be easier to turn the town upside down from the Mark Hopkins."

Carrie and Emma laughed. "Sam," Carrie said, "you're totally incorrigible!"

"And proud of it!" Sam retorted. "Now lemme go. I've got to get some shut-eye." She turned and headed back to her seat. Emma lingered a couple of minutes to tell Carrie about how Sam had put the lid on the obnoxious guys in the back of the plane, and then she, too, went back to find her seat. It wasn't long before all three girls were lulled to sleep by the vibration of the speeding airplane.

* * *

"Sam!" Emma whispered, tapping her friend on the arm. "We're here!"

Sam opened her eyes and looked around groggily. *We're here? Where's here?* she wondered. And then it all came back to her. *It's San Francisco. I'm about to see my birth mother again and her family. Omigod, I'm really, really nervous.*

"Are you ready for this?" Emma asked, seeing the anxious look in Sam's opening eyes.

"Ready as I'll ever be," Sam said, watching the runway roll past slowly under the plane's wheels. "Susan told me on the phone that she's meeting me by herself, so at least I won't get mobbed all at once."

"You're going to do great," Emma assured her as the plane came to a stop.

"This is it!" Sam said, mustering as much enthusiasm as she could. "C'mon, let's meet up with Carrie inside." They hustled off the plane before the obnoxious guys who'd been chanting for beer could harass them further.

When they walked through the jetway into their arrival gate, however, they were greeted not by Carrie, but by a huge hoard of photographers, television cameras and newspaper reporters. Evidently, word had leaked that Graham Perry was arriving by commercial airline, and every media-type in the San Francisco Bay area had turned out to greet him.

"Look!" Sam shouted. "There's Graham! They've got him surrounded!" She pointed over to a corner of the arrival area, where a huge crush of reporters had surrounded Graham, Claudia, Ian, little four-year-old Chloe, and Carrie. They were firing flash-bulbs and questions relentlessly.

"Graham! Over here!"

"Graham! Just one picture, just one!"

"Graham, is it true that you're still using cocaine?"

"Graham, who's the teen girl—a new girlfriend?"

"Graham, Graham, Graham!"

The crush was endless. Finally, airport security moved in, and hustled the Templetons and Carrie away, back out onto the runway and into a waiting limousine parked there. The last that Sam and Emma heard from Carrie was a shouted "Meet you guys at the hotel!" Then she was gone.

"Wow, that was unbelievable!" Sam said, as she and Emma walked down to the baggage claim area, and to Susan.

"Yes, it's terrible," Emma agreed, shaking her head.

"Terrible? I thought it was fabulous!" Sam exclaimed, practically dancing down the walkway. "Photographers, reporters, fame—that's me in about five years. No, make it three years. Two if I get the right breaks." Emma cracked up. Sam kept up her joking as they walked past the security area and metal detectors into the main airport terminal.

"Sam?" said a soft voice from the side. Sam turned to the sound of a voice. It was a small, plumpish, sort of hippie-looking woman. It was Sam's birth mother, Susan Briarly.

"Hi," Sam said, walking over to Susan. She was suddenly overwhelmed with shyness, so she just stood there.

"I'm so glad you're here," Susan said. She reached up and hugged Sam warmly.

"Susan," Sam said, pulling Emma over by her arm, "this is one of my two best friends in the world, Emma Cresswell."

Susan smiled broadly at Emma and stuck out her hand, which Emma took and shook.

"I've seen you perform," Susan said easily, "when you were up on stage with Sam and that rock band back in Maine."

"Oh," Emma said, grateful that they had something light to talk about, "you mean Flirting with Danger. That was a fun night."

"You both were very good," Susan said sincerely. "I can't sing a note myself, but Sam's father had a wonderful voice. He was actually a part-time cantor."

"A cantor?" Sam asked, puzzled.

"The man who leads the singing at Jewish religious services," Susan explained.

Wow, Sam thought. *I've got a lot to learn about myself.*

Susan, Sam and Emma kept up an easy banter as they went and gathered their few bags and walked outside to Susan's Volvo wagon. When they put their bags inside, Sam could see a bumper sticker that read "Lobotomies for Republicans: It's the Law" on the back of the car. *Yep, an old hippie,* Sam thought. Susan pulled the car out of the lot and turned it north on Highway 101 towards San Francisco. Though the sun was shining brightly, Sam could see banks of fog out the left window spilling over the hills.

"You sure you two don't want to stay with me and my family?" Susan asked. "It's a lot less expensive than the Mark Hopkins Hotel!" Sam knew Susan was right—that the Mark Hopkins was one of the most expensive hotels in town.

"Uh, Emma's family has a special arrangement with them, so it's no trouble at all," Sam lied. *Yeah, right. Special arrangement. She arranges to hand them her credit card and they arrange to give her a suite!*

"Okay," Susan said, keeping her eyes on the road. "So I'll drop you off at the hotel and you can maybe catch up on your sleep. Then how about if I pick both of you up, and this friend Carrie that Sam told me about, and I take you to Oakland to meet the family and have dinner? Say, about six o'clock?"

"That's fine," Sam told Susan. But as she stared out the window and watched the streets of San Francisco rolling by, one word stuck in her head. Family. She was going to meet some complete strangers who were her family. And most terrifying of all, she was going to meet Susan's husband, Carson, the man who had never wanted Sam to even exist.

SIX

Late that afternoon, Emma, Sam and Carrie all sat lost in thought in the California sun in a small park across the street from the Mark Hopkins. They were listening to the clanging bells of the cable cars as they rolled past them on California Street. Ian and Chloe Templeton were flying a kite they had bought in the hotel gift shop.

Sam was thinking about her up coming meeting with Carson, Carrie was thinking about the letter she'd written to Josh, and Emma was thinking about Kurt's 'let's-be-engaged-to-be-engaged' proposal.

Sam looked over at her two friends, who both seemed to be staring out at nothing. "Hey, fellow-foxes!" Sam called to them. "We are here in gorgeous San Francisco, so let's stop thinking so much!"

"You're right," Carrie agreed. "Let's just have fun."

"I agree," Emma said firmly. They all watched the kids with their kite. "Remember when life used to be that easy?" Emma added wistfully.

"Hey, it basically sucks to be a kid," Sam reminded her friends. "You have no rights at all, remember?"

"I suppose," Emma agreed. "But don't those kids look worry-free to you?"

"Well, their father is a rich and famous rock star; that helps," Sam pointed out. She watched the batlike kite swoop against the afternoon sky, "Pretty cool to be flying a kite in the middle of the city."

"Wouldn't be too cool," Carrie replied, "if we suddenly got shook by an earthquake." She looked down at her feet and grinned because they were both safely on the ground.

"Earthquake!" Sam exclaimed. "I forgot all about them. They have them here, right?"

"I was in one once," Emma said, turning her face up to the sun. "But not here. In Turkey, where I was traveling with my parents." *The trip with my parents was*

98

worse than the earthquake, Emma remembered.

"What was it like?" Sam asked.

"It felt kind of like our hotel had been run into by a truck," Emma explained. "It was scary, but kind of exciting, too."

"Speaking of exciting," Carrie asked, keeping a watchful eye on Ian and Chloe, "how did Kurt feel about your coming out here with us?"

Emma sighed. "Well, he said he didn't mind."

"That's cool," Sam said.

"He was really nice about it," Emma added.

"He's a great guy," Carrie said.

"But then he suggested that we get engaged to get engaged," Emma qualified.

"He *what?!*" Sam screeched.

"He said that he loved me more than anything in the world and said that we ought to think about getting serious," Emma repeated.

"Wow," Carrie breathed.

"How could you go all this time without telling us?" Sam cried. "This is mega-big news!"

Emma shrugged and stared at the kite high in the sky.

"So," Carrie asked reasonably, "how do you feel about it?"

"I don't know," Emma replied truthfully. "All mixed up. Sort of like Sam feels about meeting her birth family." She managed a small smile.

"Now don't go and change the subject on us, Emma Cresswell," Sam mock-scolded her. "You are the first one of us to get a marriage proposal, and you're not worming out of it that easily."

"It wasn't a proposal, Sam," Emma said evenly.

"Yes it was," Sam said, reaching her left hand forward and extending her bare ring finger out like a bride on the altar.

"I love him," Emma said. "I know I love him, but . . ."

"Yeah, it's the 'but' part," Carrie commiserated. "It's one of the reasons I had to finally break up with Josh. He wanted more of a commitment than I was ready to give."

"Not the same at all!" Sam protested. "You wanted to be free to see other guys, whereas Emma knows Kurt is her one and only true love, forever and ever, amen, right, Em?"

"Right," Emma agreed, but her voice didn't sound quite so certain.

"Well, when it comes to guys I am definitely not ready for happily-ever-after," Sam said, kicking at a stone at her feet. "But I can understand feeling—I don't know—conflicted, I guess you'd call it."

"Me too," Carrie nodded.

"It's like how I feel about this whole trip," Sam said earnestly. "I'm going to meet my birth mother's husband and my adopted brother and half-sister in about an hour, and while part of me really wants to do it, part of me wants to just go hide in the hotel room."

"That's natural, Sam," Carrie said. "I had a hard enough time just writing my letter to Josh."

"What are you most afraid of, Sam?" Emma asked.

Sam fidgeted uncomfortably before she answered. "I don't know," she said. "That they won't like me. That I won't like them. That I'll end up without either a birth mother or a natural mother. That they'll like me too much. You name it, I'm afraid of it."

"Yeah," Carrie agreed.

"You said it," Emma nodded.

Carrie looked at her watch. "Well, now that we've all agreed that we're the three most chicken girls on the planet, we better get back to the hotel, because Susan is coming to get us in a half hour."

"I'm really glad you're coming, too, Carrie. I'll take all the moral support I can get."

"You got it," Carrie assured her, getting up from the bench. "Besides, it'll give Graham and Claudia a chance to be alone with the kids tonight. Between rehearsal and the show, tomorrow is going to be nuts."

Carrie had only a little difficulty getting Chloe to give up the kite string, and soon all three girls and both kids were walking back to the Mark Hopkins.

Towards what, Sam couldn't be sure.

"Wow, this is the famous Haight-Ashbury?" Sam exclaimed, swiveling her head so she could look out the window of Susan's Volvo. "My parents have a book about this place!"

102

Sam was sitting in the front seat, Carrie and Emma were in the back, and Susan was giving them a quick tour of San Francisco—"the ten-cent tour," she called it—before driving them over the Bay Bridge to her home in Oakland. They'd already driven through Chinatown and down Lombard Street, "the crookedest street in the world," which wound down a hillside like a stretched-out toy Slinky.

Susan smiled. "There was a lot of history made here in the late sixties. Can you picture both sides of this street lined with kids with long hair, love beads, no shoes, tie-dyed shirts, and bell-bottoms?"

Sam grimaced. "Long hair, yes. Love beads, maybe. Tie-dye, okay. But bell-bottoms? Huge fashion error!"

"I agree!" Susan said with a laugh. "And you guys look great, I might add."

Sam had chosen a casual outfit for the dinner with her family—a faded blue denim workshirt with leopard–print cuffs (which she'd added herself) and a pair of faded jeans tucked into her trademark red cowboy boots. Carrie had on baggy, white cotton pants and an oversized red-and-white striped rugby shirt, and Emma wore a raspberry-colored short pleated skirt with a pink sleeveless T-shirt and her lace and denim jean jacket.

"Right here," Susan said, pointing to the corner of Haight and Ashbury streets, "it was all happening. This was the hippie center of the universe. Did you know that a whole bunch of kids met here, formed a huge school bus caravan, and headed off to form a commune in Tennessee?"

"No kidding?" Sam marveled. "That sounds way cool."

"Yup," Susan continued, "it's called The Farm, and it's still around. I even know Stephen Gaskin, who founded it and led the kids out there—and I know some people who still live there." Her voice trailed off wistfully.

"So, were you were a hippie, too?" Carrie asked.

"Still am," Susan answered, smiling as they passed the corner of Haight and Stanyan streets, and turned left to head up towards Parnassus Heights. "Only now I have a regular job instead of selling underground newspapers, and I hardly smoke marijuana anymore."

Hello! Sam thought to herself. *Here I am*

tooling around San Francisco with my birth mother, and she's telling me that not only did she hang out in the Haight–Ashbury when she was in college, but she also smoked—correction, still smokes—marijuana. My adopted parents would be so pleased! Actually, they'd be horrified.

"Weren't you afraid of the police?" Carrie asked.

"What I was most afraid of," and here Sam could see that Susan got a faraway look in her eyes, "was that my friends would get drafted, sent to Vietnam and killed."

"Vietnam, because of the war?" Sam asked.

"Yes," Susan said, "And it was a bad war. And friends did get sent there. And were killed. Listen, let's talk about Vietnam another time. Don't get me started. Look here. I want to show you something." The Volvo slowed as they passed the corner of Moraga Street and Fourteenth Avenue.

Susan parked the Volvo, got out of the car and motioned for the girls to follow her. She started climbing a long stairway up a hillside that seemed to Sam to go on forever. Finally, they got to the top.

"This is called Grandview Park," Susan said. "Not many people know about it."

"Grand view is right," Carrie said. "This is amazing. Look, you can even see the Golden Gate Bridge from here. And look there—there's Golden Gate Park. And what's that big church across the way?"

"That's St. Ignatius Church," Susan said informatively. "It's on the campus of the University of San Francisco." She looked down at her watch. "Oh wow, look at the time," she said. "I told them all we'd be back by seven-thirty and it's already seven. Let's hit the road."

Susan and the girls climbed back down the stairway to the car. Once they were in, Susan turned the Volvo around and headed for Oakland.

Sam looked around the modest, but tastefully decorated living room. *I can't believe I'm sitting here drinking a Coke in my birth mother's living room,* she thought incredulously. *It's like a scene from a movie.* She looked over at Sam and Carrie, who were sitting side by side on the couch, and could tell that they were thinking the same thing. *I'm so glad they're here,* Sam thought. *I don't know if I could handle this without them.*

Most of the family was there, too. Sitting directly across from Emma and Carrie was Susan's husband, Carson. Susan had described Carson as a good father but a by-the-book kind of guy, and Sam thought she had gotten that right. He worked as an internal auditor for the city of Oakland, and while Sam had no idea what an auditor did, Carson looked like what she thought an auditor should look like: sandy hair, slight build, brown eyes, about five foot eight, not exactly bad-looking, but hardly handsome. *Hey, maybe I'm just being hard on him because I'm sure he hates me,* Sam admitted to herself, studying Carson out of the corner of her eye.

"Your daughter looks just like you," Emma said politely.

"A lot of people say that," Susan said with a smile, lovingly stroking the baby's hair.

"Would anyone like anything else to drink?" Carson asked, standing up. No one said anything. "In that case, I've got some work to do upstairs before dinner." He looked around. No one said anything. He left.

"He brings a lot of his work home," Susan said apologetically.

"Whatever," Sam said, sipping her Coke as if she couldn't care less.

Carrie shot Sam a supportive look. *Don't let him get to you,* the look seemed to say.

Wow, Emma thought, *I thought maybe Sam was being paranoid, but maybe she's right—Susan's husband really doesn't like her!* "It must be interesting, editing children's books," Emma said graciously, anxious to smooth over the awkward moment.

"Hello all!" a cheery baritone voice rang out from the front hall. "Is she here?"

"That's Adam, your brother," Sam's birth mother told Sam.

My brother, Sam repeated in her mind. *That is just too weird-sounding.*

Adam rounded the corner and all three girls stood up, stunned.

No one who looks that good can be anyone's brother, Carrie thought.

That's my brother? Sam thought.

But it was Emma who really lost it, although being Emma, no one else could tell. As she stared at Adam's thick black hair, green eyes and tall, rangy, muscular build, she thought, *This is the most hand-*

some guy I've ever seen in my entire life,
and I should be kissing him right this
instant.

She was only glad that no one could read her mind.

SEVEN

"This chicken is great," Carrie said, swallowing another bite of coq au vin. "Did you really cook this?"

"I did," Susan said with a smile. "And I'd be embarrassed to tell you how easy it was to make."

"Do you like it?" Adam asked, his eyes on Emma.

"Oh yes, it's excellent," Emma replied. She could feel herself blushing like some stupid school girl. *Listen, Emma,* she told herself, *snap out of it. Just because the best-looking guy you've ever seen in your life is sitting across from you, and just because he seems to be as attracted to you as you are to him, is no reason to act like a fool.*

111

"Sarah seems to like it, too," Sam said, watching the baby gum a piece of meat.

"She's such a sweetheart," Susan said, fondly brushing the little girl's lock of curly hair off her face.

Sam felt a pang somewhere near her heart. That baby was her sister. And her sister was getting the love and attention from Susan that she'd never gotten herself. It didn't seem right. It didn't seem fair.

"So, tell us about Kansas," Susan urged Sam.

"Well, it's not exactly the entertainment capital of the world, but I managed to keep it hopping," Sam said. She launched into a story about one of her wilder adventures.

Susan seemed to hang on her every word, but Carson looked more and more uncomfortable.

"I'll go give Sarah her bath," Carson said, abruptly getting up from the table and lifting the baby into his arms. "Excuse me."

There was a moment of awkward silence after Carson left the room.

"Gee, I didn't know he hated the Midwest so much," Sam finally quipped.

"Hey, ignore Dad," Adam told Sam. "I, for one, am really glad you're here."

Which implies Carson isn't, Sam said to herself, gulping hard. *Like it isn't patently obvious.*

"Would you like more wine?" Adam asked Emma, ready to pour more into her glass.

"No, thanks," Emma said, covering her glass with her hand. *Who knows what I might do if I have another glass of wine,* she thought giddily, and then felt incredibly guilty at the fickleness of her thoughts. *This is nuts! I simply can't feel this way!*

"We can go into the living room for coffee and dessert," Susan suggested, getting up from the table.

"Mmmm, dessert," Sam rhapsodized, "one of my favorite words."

"Mine too!" Susan said with delight, clearly pleased at any similarities between them.

"That perfume is incredible," Adam murmured to Emma as he walked by her.

"I'm not wearing any," Emma replied, her voice sounding strained to her own ears. *Why does he keep staring at me like that?* she asked herself. *Everyone is going to notice!*

When the girls and Adam had found seats, Susan brought in a homemade lemon cheesecake and a carafe of coffee. She told them a story while they were eating about how she had actually met two of the Beatles years ago when they were in San Francisco.

"Who're the Beatles?" Carrie asked jokingly.

Sam hooted. "They're the band Paul McCartney was in before he was in Wings."

"God, do I feel old," Susan laughed. "Believe me, you guys missed the greatest era in music."

"Don't get her started or she'll drag out her old Bob Dylan albums," Adam said, getting up. "How about if I drive you back to the Mark Hopkins?" he asked, looking at Emma. "The view from the Bay Bridge at night is gorgeous, and I'd like to be the one to show it to . . . all of you." Carrie and Sam looked over at Emma—it was pretty clear he was really talking to her.

"It's really nice of you to offer, Adam," Susan said. The look in her eye said she had caught on to his attraction to Emma, but she wasn't about to say anything.

114

"Dinner was incredible," Sam told Susan, searching for her purse.

"Can we help clean up?" Carrie asked.

"Absolutely not," Susan said. "I'll just shove this stuff into the dishwasher. Sam, you'll call me tomorrow morning?" Susan asked, anxiously.

"Sure thing," Sam replied, "but not too early. I don't consider anything before ten o'clock actually the morning."

"I hate mornings, too!" Susan said, smiling happily at Sam.

"Thanks for dinner, Susan," Carrie said politely, as she hoisted her purse strap over her shoulder.

"Oh yes, thank you for dinner," Emma added. *Omigosh, I almost forgot to thank her. What is happening to me?* She put on her jean jacket and caught Adam looking at her again. *Just ignore it, she told herself. So he's cute. Big deal.*

Sam went over and hugged Susan. "Thanks, Susan," she said. "Thanks for everything." Susan's face lit up like a little child's on Christmas morning.

The girls and Adam all left Susan's house and piled into Adam's convertible—it was an old restored Volkswagen bug that Adam said he did the work on himself.

"What's the license plate mean?" Emma asked, pointing to the vanity plate on the car that read "FADE IN."

"It's a film term," Adam answered. "It's the first words that start any screenplay. At that point, there's always hope. Just like in love." He looked right at Emma, laughed to himself, backed the VW out of the driveway and headed for San Francisco.

"Yes!" Sam screamed out into the night air, as they crossed over San Francisco Bay. "I love it here!"

In the back, Emma and Carrie were bouncing along to a hot Mary Chapin Carpenter song on the radio. "I love country music," Adam shouted above the wind, looking at Emma in the rearview mirror. "How about you guys?"

"Hate it!" Carrie yelled.

"Sucks!" Sam added.

"They're kidding," Emma clarified.

"Good," Adam said with a laugh, and cranked the radio up even louder.

The radio switched to a set of all Garth Brooks songs, and the girls and Adam all sang along in the open car until Adam pulled into the circular driveway in front of the Mark Hopkins.

"Hey, I have a great idea," Carrie said, as they stopped in front of the hotel.

"What's that?" Adam said, still casting glances at Emma in the rearview mirror.

"Well, remember I told you at dinner that I work for Graham Perry," Carrie said slowly, a plan unfolding in her mind, "and you know he's playing this big show tomorrow night—"

"Sounds like a great job," Adam said.

"It is," Carrie agreed. "Anyway, I was thinking . . ."

"Yes!" Sam interrupted. "You want Adam to get two incredibly cute friends and we'll all go to the show together. And you'll get us in!"

"Sam!" Carrie exclaimed.

"Well," Sam countered, "isn't that what you were going to say?"

"Yes," Carrie admitted, "but you could at least let me enjoy saying it!"

"I think it's a great idea," Adam said. "Don't you, Emma?"

"Fine," Emma said cooly, trying not to stare back into Adam's huge, green eyes.

117

"Then it's set," Adam said. "We can talk logistics tomorrow morning."

"Thanks for the ride," Carrie said as the girls got out of the car.

"No problem," Adam assured her. "It was great meeting you, Sam," he added warmly.

"Thanks," Sam said, a big grin on her face. "I really mean it."

"Well, it was nice to have met you," Emma told Adam, reverting out of sheer nervousness to the overly proper way she used to talk. She reached her hand out to Adam automatically.

As the other girls started toward the hotel Adam took her hand. "Nice to have met you, too," he said softly. "Now, find some way to come back out here. I'll be waiting by that corner." He indicated the intersection of California and Pine streets with his eyes.

Emma's heart pounded in her chest. "I can't do that!" she whispered.

"I'll be waiting," he said in a low voice, and took off.

Emma followed her friends into the hotel. *No Emma, you are not going to make up some excuse, sneak back outside, go for a*

118

drive with some guy you barely know, and then feel terrible about it afterwards. You are going to go upstairs, take out your diary, and write about your feelings instead. Because you are going to be loyal to Kurt. She thought this all to herself as she entered the lobby.

"Uh, Sam?" Emma heard herself saying, as she passed the hotel gift shop where Sam was looking in the window.

"God, look at these postcards," Sam said, pointing at some particularly hideous cards in the window featuring girls in bikinis with guys leering at them. "Mondo-tacky!"

"I don't know about you guys, but I'm beat," Carrie said, yawning. "I'm going to bed."

"I think I'm going to go in and . . . buy a book," Emma said distantly. "I'll see you in the morning."

"Okay," Sam said easily, "I may go up to the club at the top of the hotel and break a few hearts. See you when I see you!"

Emma was alone. *Now Emma,* she scolded herself, *go inside and buy a book, take it upstairs, and read! Forget about Adam!*

And that is exactly what she intended to

do. So Emma was astonished to find her own feet leaving the gift shop, walking through the hotel lobby, and leading her out into the night air.

Two hours later, Adam and Emma were sitting in the front seats of Adam's VW. They were parked at the top of someplace that Adam called Mount Sutro, and Emma was looking out at one of the most magnificent sights she had ever seen in her life.

"This is one of the really great places," Adam said, "and still a lot of people don't know it's here."

"You can see everything!" Emma said.

And it was true. It looked like the whole Bay Area was at their feet. To the right, Emma could see the planes queued up to land at SFX, while straight ahead—actually straight ahead and down—lay downtown San Francisco. Off to the left, Adam said, were the Sunset and Richmond residential districts of the city.

"I come up here for inspiration," Adam said, sighing contentedly. "I mean, who wouldn't be inspired by this?" He spread his hands wide as if he's created the whole thing.

"The lights remind me of the Mother Ship in *Close Encounters of the Third Kind,*" Emma said, mentioning a movie that she liked a lot.

"Spielberg," Adam said. "Richard Dreyfuss was great in that. But I prefer French cinema myself."

"You do?" Emma said.

"Absolutely," Adam said. "Miou-Miou, Isabelle Huppert, Depardieu—they can act rings around most Americans. And if I could one day direct a movie like François Truffaut . . ." his voice trailed off wistfully.

Huppert. Depardieu. Truffaut! Emma knew all the names Adam was mentioning, because she'd seen all their movies, and she didn't even need subtitles to understand them. *Kurt doesn't know anything about any of these people,* she found herself thinking for a moment, and then guiltily she banished thoughts of Kurt from her mind.

"Truffaut was my favorite director," Emma said softly.

"I was so bummed out when he died," Adam said passionately. "I suppose that sounds crazy to you—"

121

"Oh, no!" Emma insisted. "I felt that way when I heard Jane Goodall died—"

"The ethologist who worked with apes?" Adam asked with surprise.

Emma nodded earnestly. "I've always been interested in Africa and primates, and I thought she was just the greatest ethologist. She inspired this dream I have of joining the Peace Corps. . . ."

"Because you want to do something that matters, you want to affect people, right?" Adam asked.

Emma nodded and stared out at the beautiful lights. "Yes, I do. I really do."

"Me too," Adam agreed. "I finish with film school in two more years. Then, I am going to direct something as important to the world as *Small Change* or *The Last Metro.*"

"*The Last Metro* was Truffaut's last movie before he died," Emma recalled. "I loved that movie."

Adam smiled at her in the moonlight and traced the edge of her cheek with his finger. Emma held her breath.

"Enough about movies and me," Adam said quietly. "One of the worst things about the movie business is that everyone just talks about themselves. You talk."

"About what?" Emma asked.

"Anything," Adam replied. "Art. Politics. Theater. Music. What is was like growing up."

His hand was caressing her hair, and Emma loved it and hated it at the same time. *I shouldn't be doing this,* she told herself. "I'll talk if you drive," she said lightly.

"You got it," he said easily, and turned the key in the ignition.

Somehow Emma, who usually hated talking about herself and her background, started telling Adam what it was like to be the daughter of Kat and Brent Cresswell, rich grown-ups who acted like ten-year-olds. She didn't even notice where Adam was driving, until the sound of crashing surf and ocean breakers got her attention.

"Where are we?" she asked, as Adam stopped the car.

"Ocean Beach," Adam answered. "The Pacific Ocean. Follow me." He led Emma down a narrow staircase to the base of some rocks, where they could hear the sound of seals barking some distance out to sea. It was an unusually warm evening, and the seals were active. Emma laughed with delight as Adam imitated their noises.

"Sit down," Adam said.

"Where?" Emma asked, puzzled.

"Right here," he answered, spreading a blanket he had taken out of his car right on the sand at the base of the rocks. *Okay, I am going to sit down but there is no way I am going to kiss him,* Emma told herself.

She sat down. Adam sat beside her. For a long while, they said nothing, their arms brushing against one another. To Emma, it seemed as if there were electric sparks flying back and forth between their barely-touching bodies.

Then Adam kissed her. Wordlessly. Gently. And Emma never wanted the kiss to end.

"I wanted to do that from the first moment I saw you," Adam admitted in a low voice.

"Did you?" Emma said faintly.

"I pictured it over and over in my mind," he told her. "How you would feel, and smell, and taste . . ."

"And?" Emma asked.

"And it's even better than my very vivid

124

imagination," Adam said, and then he kissed her again.

They spent the night at the base of the rocks near the Cliff House, talking and kissing and holding each other, sharing what was in their hearts and minds. Somehow it just seemed right, as if they'd known each other forever.

"I can't believe we just met," Emma murmured, snuggling against Adam.

"We didn't," Adam said. "We've known each other a long, long time."

The light began to dawn in the distance. Emma could sea the seals cavorting out in the Pacific. With the light came reality. Kurt. The guy she loved.

What am I going to do? Emma thought desperately. *And how am I ever going to face Kurt again?*

EIGHT

Sam awoke the next morning to find that the efficient Mark Hopkins staff had already placed a tray holding the Sunday edition of the *San Francisco Chronicle*, a pot of coffee and some unbelievable looking muffins and breads just outside her door.

As she was moving the tray to the stand near the bed, the phone rang in her room.

"Hello?"

"Hi Sam, it's Susan," came her birth mother's voice. "I hope I didn't wake you."

"Nope, I was just going to call you, anyway," Sam told her, pouring herself a cup of coffee.

"How about if we have brunch?" Susan asked. "I could pick you up in about an hour?"

"Sounds great," Sam said. "How should I dress?"

Susan laughed. "Sam, this is California. There is only a choice of trendily casual or casually trendy."

"Gotcha," Sam agreed. "See you soon."

Sam laid back down on the huge bed and sipped the fragrant coffee. Then she bit into one of the freshly baked muffins. *This is how I was meant to live,* she told herself with satisfaction.

Then she grabbed her robe and padded over to the door that led to Emma's room, carrying her coffee with her. To Sam's surprise, Emma was still in bed, sound asleep.

"Emma-bo-bemma!" Sam whispered at her loudly.

Emma slowly rolled over. "Mmm?" she mumbled.

"Get up!" Sam said. "No San Francisco sleepyheads allowed!"

"Uh-uh," Emma grunted, then pulled the blankets over her head.

"Come on," Sam urged, "Have coffee with me before Susan comes."

"Go away," came Emma's muffled voice from under the blankets.

Sam had no choice but to retreat to her room. *Weird,* she thought. *Emma is always the one forcing me out of bed!*

Sam showered, washed and blew dry her hair, then stood in front of the closet, trying to decide what to wear. She finally picked out a long see-through skirt with black leggings underneath, a man's paisley vest and her red cowboy boots. Then she wrote a quick note and slipped it under Emma's door.

Yo, Sleeper!
    Susan's taking me out for brunch. I tried to wake you but you were basically in a coma. We'll be back here in the early aft. And you'd better be awake to come with us then. So I'm telling the front desk to ring you at noon! Hey, what are friends for?

Sam signed the note by quickly sketching a cowboy boot at the bottom of the page. Then she looked at the clock. It was ten o'clock—time to meet Susan down in the lobby.

Sam gave herself a final once-over in the bathroom's full-length mirror. *Not bad,* she thought. *Not bad for a farm girl from Kansas.* At the last minute she picked up her red felt hat with the flowers in the front that she'd bought just before she'd left the island, and she stuck it on her head. "Babe-alicious," she told her reflection. "Who wouldn't love you?"

"Hi!" she called to Susan when she got off the elevator. Susan was looking in the window of the gift shop.

"Hi there," Susan said. "You look great!"

"Thanks," Sam said with a grin.

"Did you see these sexist postcards in the window?" Susan asked with disgust, pointing to the same girls-in-bikinis postcards Sam had pointed out to Emma.

"Yeah, I thought they were incredibly tacky," Sam said. "But maybe it's supposed to be some kind of retro thing."

"Meaning?" Susan asked, her eyebrows raised.

Sam shrugged. "I don't know—like, so tacky that it's hip, that kind of thing."

"I don't get it," Susan said bluntly.

"Well, they look like they're from the fifties or something," Sam explained. "I mean, cartoons of guys drooling over girls in bikinis? Come on now!"

Susan looked at Sam thoughtfully. "You know, women of my generation fought really hard for the rights of women, and women of your generation just take it for granted."

"I don't really give it much thought, to tell you the truth," Sam said, the new *Vogue* magazine catching her eye.

"Well, that's exactly my point," Susan said. "You ready to go?"

"Just a sec," Sam said, and walked over to the front desk to tell the clerk to place a wake-up call to their suite at noon.

"What's that all about?" Susan asked, joining Sam at the front desk.

"Oh, Emma's still sleeping—guess she had a rough night," Sam joked. "I just wanted her to be awake for lunch."

A worried look crossed Susan's face. "I hope it wasn't anything I cooked for her!"

"Naah," Sam replied, rubbing her stomach. "I ate twice as much as Emma, and the same food she ate, and I feel fine. Speaking of food, where's breakfast?"

"I thought we'd go to the Grand Piano on Haight Street," Susan said. "It's kind of a landmark. You ready?"

Sam nodded and started walking toward

131

the front doors of the hotel. "One thing you'll learn about me," she said confidentially to Susan, "is that I'm always ready for a good meal. And Carrie hates me because I never gain any weight."

Susan laughed. "Well, the appetite part you might have inherited from me, but the metabolism you definitely inherited from your father."

My father. Michael Blady. Some Israeli guy I never met, maybe never will meet. Life is so strange. Sam thought about the photo of Michael that Susan had given her when she visited Sunset Island. It showed a tall, handsome, muscular but lanky, redheaded man, smiling confidently at the camera. Sam had carried it in her wallet ever since.

They got into Susan's Volvo which was parked outside and Susan drove them back to the Haight–Ashbury district. There was a spot right in front of the Grand Piano, and Susan pulled into it.

"Wait'll you see this place," Susan said. "It hasn't changed much since I was a teenager."

"Can't wait," Sam said, "as long as they serve food."

But even Sam wasn't ready for what she

saw when they walked in the door. It looked like the set from a movie about the 1960s. There were tapestries covering the walls, as well as old anti-war posters from the Vietnam War era. None of the tables and chairs matched. The place was half-full, and people were not only eating breakfast there, but were also playing chess, reading books, and just hanging out.

Whoa, baby, Sam thought to herself. *I'm in a time warp. The only thing that's out of place is that there's classical music coming over the sound system instead of Janis Joplin or Jimi Hendrix.*

"So what do you think?" Susan said, as she steered Sam to a quiet table in the corner.

Sam looked around, and then a wide grin spread over her face. "It's great," she said truthfully. "But where's Bob Dylan? I thought he was supposed to meet us here!"

"Oh, you guys are ganging up on me. Adam teases me about Dylan all the time!" Susan laughed.

"Well, come on," Sam said. "You have to admit, Dylan sounded like a car honking at the bottom of the ocean!"

"I am cut to the quick," Susan said

dramatically. "He was the master poet of his time."

A waitress dressed in hippie regalia came over and took their order—Susan ordered a cup of tea, poached eggs and a bran muffin. Sam ordered orange juice, a three-cheese omelette, home fries, bacon, and a bagel on the side.

"Where do you put it?" Susan marveled.

"Hollow leg," Sam answered solemnly.

Susan looked startled for a moment. "That's what he used to say."

"Who used to say that?"

"Your father," Susan said. "He used to use that very expression."

Sam sipped her coffee, her face troubled. "Susan, I wish you wouldn't call him 'my father'," Sam said. "I have a father back in Kansas."

"I understand," Susan said. "I'll just refer to him as Michael. How's that?"

"Okay," Sam agreed, not knowing what else to say. For a few moments, the only sound at their table was a Bach harpsichord piece playing over the Grand Piano sound system. *Can I ask her about him? Okay what the hell—that's why I'm here,* Sam thought.

"What was he . . . Michael . . . really like?" Sam finally asked.

Susan got the faraway look in her eyes again. "I told you he was the most handsome man in the world, right?"

Sam nodded.

"He was also brilliant," Susan continued. "He was in the Israeli Army intelligence division, because he spoke Arabic perfectly, as well as Hebrew and English."

Sam's jaw opened in astonishment. *Intelligence?* "He was a spy?"

Susan smiled. "He didn't talk to me much about what he did in the army. But I gathered that he spent a lot of time figuring out coded transmissions from Syria."

"Tell me about his family," Sam urged.

"They were Jews from Oslo, Norway," Susan said. "Holocaust survivors."

"Holocaust?" Sam asked in shock. "You mean they were in one of Hitler's concentration camps?"

Susan nodded. "They survived Auschwitz. Fifteen hundred from Oslo were sent there—fifty survived. It was a miracle they made it through."

Sam was dumbfounded. *My father is the*

child of two people who were in the Nazi concentration camps. And Norwegian.

"It's, it's . . . incredible," Sam stammered. "I didn't even know that there were Jews in Norway."

"There aren't many now," Susan said, taking a sip of water, "but before the war there were a few thousand. Hey, there are Jews all over the world. Even in Africa."

"You're kidding!" Sam said.

"No, I'm serious," Susan assured her. "There are black Jews in Ethiopia. Of course, most of them have emigrated to Israel now."

The waitress set down Sam's orange juice and Sam sipped it contemplatively. "There are hardly any Jewish families in Junction, Kansas, where I'm from," Sam said. "There was one girl in my class—she used to miss school on holidays with funny names."

"Like Rosh Hashanah—that's the Jewish new year," Susan explained.

"Well, why is it different from everybody else's new year?" Sam asked.

"Because the Jews began counting from the beginning of recorded time," Susan said, "and the Christians started over again after Jesus."

Wow. There is a lot I don't know about myself, Sam thought for about the fifth time since she'd arrived in San Francisco. *This is kind of cool, actually. I'm a minority!*

"So you really don't know what happened to Michael after you came back to the United States?" Sam asked. *Maybe she knows something and just didn't want to tell me the first time she met me.*

"Not really," Susan said, sadly staring down at the table.

The waitress came and put their breakfasts on the table in front of them.

"Does 'not really' mean no, you know nothing or does it mean you know something but you don't want to tell me?" Sam asked bluntly, taking a bite out of her bagel.

Susan smiled. "You're not very diplomatic. Did you know that?"

"Yeah," Sam replied. "And you don't have to tell me if you don't want to."

"I never actually heard from Michael again after I left Israel," Susan said slowly. "Well, as I told you, I wrote to him and told

137

him it was over, and then that was that. But I got a letter from his parents—they were still alive—in the early 1980s."

"His parents wrote to you?" Sam asked with surprise.

"Michael had told them all about me," Susan said. "They said Michael had been on a mission in Lebanon and was missing. They thought I'd want to know." Sam saw tears well up in Susan's eyes.

"And that's the last you heard?" Sam whispered.

Susan nodded. "Please Sam," Susan urged, "never mention this letter to Adam or Carson."

"I won't," Sam promised. But in her mind was the question she couldn't bring herself to ask: *When Michael's parents wrote to you, why didn't you write back to tell them they have a granddaughter?*

When Susan and Sam arrived back at the hotel, Emma was waiting for them in the lobby. She was wearing jeans, a black turtleneck tank top and large sunglasses.

"Don't you look like a movie star," Sam joked, "and you're sleeping late like a movie star, too."

"A French movie star," Emma replied in a fake French accent. That remark reminded Emma of Adam—as if she needed reminding.

"Have you been to the Top of the Mark yet?" Susan asked Sam and Emma. Sam shook her head no—she'd been planning to go the night before, but instead ended up falling asleep from jet lag.

"I've been there," Emma said quietly, "a few times."

Susan looked surprised.

"Emma's been everywhere," Sam informed Susan. "We're talking billionaire heiress here."

"Subtlety is not Sam's long suit," Emma muttered, clearly embarrassed.

"Well, then, as Emma knows, it's pretty grand," Susan said, recovering the moment nicely. "There's a huge brunch buffet, Emma, if you're hungry, but we just ate."

"I'm not really hungry," Emma said, "but I could use a cup of tea."

"Then let's go," Susan said, leading the way to an elevator below a sign that said "Top of the Mark."

They rode the elevator to the top floor, where the elevator attendant cried out

"Top o' the Mark!" They stepped out into the most magnificent dining room Sam had ever seen. All four walls were glass, there was a 360 degree view of the Bay Area, and what struck Sam the most was the number of sailboats out on the bay itself.

A well-dressed waiter led them to a table, and in an instant had poured tea for Emma and big glasses of orange juice for Susan and Sam.

"I wanted to thank you again for dinner last night," Emma said to Susan. "It was great meeting your whole family."

"And they enjoyed meeting you," Susan said warmly. "Especially Adam, if I'm not mistaken."

She doesn't know anything, Emma thought frantically. *She couldn't know anything!* "He seems . . . quite nice," Emma said in an overly polite voice.

"Yes, Lady Di," Sam teased Emma. "And he's also a total babe!"

Susan laughed. "Yeah, he's a cutie, all right. But what's more important is, he's a really good person."

"Seems like it," Emma agreed easily.

"Emma isn't interested," Sam told Susan.

"She's completely in love with her boy-friend, Kurt Ackerman. Now, if she was anything like me, she'd go for the gusto!"

Everyone laughed, including Emma. But inside, Emma was scared. Because she knew she was acting much more like Sam than she dared to admit.

NINE

Sam lay on the bed in her hotel room staring at the ceiling. She dropped another grape into her mouth from the fruit plate she'd ordered and sighed contently.

Things were going great. Claudia had decided to get a baby-sitter for Chloe so that Ian and Carrie could go to the concert (and Carrie could take some photos). She'd even arranged for a limo, so that they could all travel in style. *What a life,* Sam thought, dropping another grape into her mouth. *The only thing missing is an incredibly buff guy to be dropping these grapes into my mouth!*

The phone rang, and Sam sat up and answered it.

"Hi, it's Adam," came her brother's voice.

"Hey, bro," Sam said breezily. Bro. *I just*

called him bro. I have a brother and this is him. It still seemed so strange. Sam had to keep reminding herself that it was true.

"Listen," Adam said, "I had an idea about the concert. How about instead of bringing two friends with me, I bring Susan? She's a big music fan, and I'm sure she'd love to come."

"Great idea!" Sam cried. *Why didn't I think of that? I mean, she only paid for me to come out here.* "Tell you what. I'll talk to Carrie and find out where we should leave backstage passes for you. Billy Joel goes on before Graham—at eight o'clock. How about you get there at seven? We can hang with the rich and famous."

"Cool," Adam agreed. "Later!" He hung up.

Sam walked over to the radio console in her room and flipped it on. "Long Live Rock!" poured out of the speakers. "Yes!" Sam exclaimed, and started dancing alone in the room to the classic sounds of The Who. *This trip is going unbelievably well,* she thought to herself. *And nothing's going to mess it up!*

Several hours later, Sam was standing with Emma, Carrie, Susan and Adam, backstage at the Oakland Coliseum before the Billy Joel/Graham Perry Earth Rock Concert for the environment, straining her ears to overhear a most remarkable conversation between Ian Templeton and a world-famous rock star.

"So Ian, how's your band coming along?" Billy Joel said to Ian Templeton, as the two of them sat next to one another on a set of wooden steps in the backstage area.

"Pretty well, Mr. Joel," Ian said, the picture of politeness. "I think we're making artistic progress."

"Ian, I told you when your band was out on my boat earlier this summer to call me *Billy*. Not Mr. Joel. *Billy*. Okay?" Billy Joel mock-scolded Graham Perry's fourteen-year-old son.

"Okay, Billy," Ian beamed.

"Have you thought about changing its name?" Billy Joel asked diplomatically. "I'm not sure that Lord Whitehead and the Zit People is the most commercially wise choice you could make."

Sam snorted back a laugh, and motioned to Carrie, Emma and the others to shush so they could listen in.

"Well, Billy," Ian said, affecting a tone of

confidentiality, "the thought has crossed my mind, but I'm going to wait until it's the right time."

"Good idea, Ian," Billy said. "Timing is everything. And now, it's time for me to get warmed up. See you after the show."

"See you, Billy," Ian said, and as Billy Joel went to warm up his voice, Sam could see that Ian was on cloud nine.

"What a great guy!" Adam marveled. "He wasn't condescending or anything."

"No, he wasn't," Emma agreed. She was standing right next to Adam and it was difficult for her to think about anything but him. "Tell them about Ian's band, Carrie," she forced herself to add.

Carrie told Susan and Adam about the evolution of the band from Lord Whitehead and the Zit Men to the all-new Lord Whitehead and the Zit People. When she was finished, both Susan and Adam were near tears from laughter.

"Hey," Adam said, "don't knock it. If Billy Ray Cyrus could become an overnight country sensation, anything can happen. This is America!" They all laughed again.

Just then one of Billy Joel's roadies announced that Billy Joel was going on

146

stage in five minutes and that his set would run about an hour. Sam, Carrie and Susan went to one section of VIP seating reserved for press and photographers, and Emma and Adam decided to check out another on the opposite side of the stage.

"This is going to be great," Adam said to Emma, leading Emma to her seat.

Emma deliberately leaned away from Adam's hand, even though it took all her willpower to do so. *Okay,* Emma thought to herself. *Last night was last night. I'm only human. It happened and I feel awful about it because of Kurt, but it's over and I'm not going to compound the problem. I'm going to accept that I'm attracted to Adam and that he's attracted to me, and that's that. That's all that's going to happen.*

Adam took Emma's hand. *No,* Emma thought to herself. *Let go of his hand. Now.* But somehow she couldn't make herself let go.

Billy Joel launched into his first number, "You May Be Right," and the entire crowd packed into the Oakland Coliseum, jumped to its feet and sang along. Adam and Emma stood on their chairs to watch Joel cavort around the stage. The song

147

ended to thunderous applause. Emma's hand was still firmly holding onto Adam's.

The two of them rocked out to Joel's tumultuous set. He finished with a cover version of Garth Brooks's "I've Got Friends In Low Places," which Emma knew because it had been such a huge crossover radio hit.

"That's hilarious!" Adam shouted to Emma over the screaming fans. "He's paying Garth back because Garth recorded his song, 'Shameless'!"

It took forever to quiet the crazed fans, but finally Billy Joel got their attention as he stood at the mike.

"Ladies and gentlemen," a sweaty, excited Billy Joel told the crowd, "I want to bring out a good friend of mine, and a good friend of the planet Earth, and one of the great heros of rock and roll . . . Mr. Graham Perry!"

The Coliseum exploded into tumultuous cheers and applause again. Graham Perry and his five-piece band ran out on stage. While the band was dressed casually, Graham had on a gorgeous Italian-cut tuxedo, with a green ribbon pinned to it to promote environmental awareness. He

grabbed the microphone and launched into
"I Run For Cover."

> "I run for cover
> Under cover of darkness
> You shine your lovelight
> With a searchlight so heartless."

Emma could see Carrie, with two cam-
eras strung around her neck, at the edge of
the stage, busily snapping action shots of
Graham. And she could see Susan and
Sam, mother and daughter, rocking out to
Graham Perry's monster hit.

Graham's set went on for nearly an hour
and a half. He ran through all his hits,
"Quick Fix," "Love's Lonely Road," "Plugged
In," and "SFX," each of which drew roars
from the crowd. Like Billy Joel, Graham's
encore was a cover tune—he performed
Billy Joel's "Only The Good Die Young,"
and midway through the song, Billy Joel,
now dressed in a Protect the Planet T-shirt
and jeans, came out and sang with him.
The crowd went wild, screaming along
with Billy and Graham, waving lit matches
and lighters so that the room looked as if it

were alive with fireflies. Then, finally, it was over.

"What a show!" Adam said to Emma, as they sank back into their seats.

"The greatest," Emma agreed. She felt Adam's arm around her shoulder and she made no effort to disengage herself.

"I am very glad you came out here with Sam," Adam said, as the arena began to grow quiet.

"Me too," Emma said, "because Sam—"

"Not just because of Sam," Adam interrupted, "because of me. I think you're the most incredible girl I've ever met in my life. So beautiful, so smart, so—"

"Much fun to talk to?" Emma finished the sentence for him. "I've never been able to talk to anyone as easily as I can talk to you," she added earnestly.

"I feel the same way," Adam told her, gently caressing her neck.

You've got to stop this! Emma told herself frantically. *You don't even know Adam, not really. What about Kurt?* Suddenly, the image of Kurt Ackerman welled up inside her, and Emma felt awful, sick to her stomach with anxiety and guilt. *What am I doing??*

"Listen, Adam," Emma said in a low voice, mustering up all her courage, "There's a problem." *Okay I'm just going to say what needs to be said. I have to do this, no matter how hard it is. Like Carrie writing to Josh.*

"Yeah, I know," Adam said. "You're going back to Sunset Island tomorrow night and—"

"It's more than that," Emma said tightly. "There's someone else."

"What?" asked Adam, not comprehending.

"There's someone else," Emma said. "Another guy. My boyfriend. His name is Kurt."

For a moment, Adam was silent. "That doesn't surprise me," Adam finally said. "It was just going too perfectly."

"Look," Emma said, "I feel awful because—"

"Don't," Adam said, "just don't feel awful."

"Why not?" Emma asked, feeling tears well up in her eyes. "I'm as confused as I've ever been in my life and you're telling me not to feel bad."

"You think you're the first person this has ever happened to?" Adam asked, his voice very soft and oddly comforting. "You think *I* don't have a girlfriend, too?"

Emma thought for a moment. *Well, that was awfully presumptuous of me, to think that he was unattached.*

"Do you?" she asked cautiously.

"Nope," he smiled ruefully.

Emma smiled back, but she still felt as if her heart were breaking.

"Look Emma, I don't know how serious you are with this other guy—"

"Serious," Emma answered honestly.

"Are you sure?" Adam asked, his eyes searching hers. "I may not have known you for very long, but I know you're not a fickle person. If things were so serious with this guy, I don't think you'd be feeling the way you feel about me."

"I . . . I don't know," Emma admitted with anguish. "I'm so confused!"

"This isn't some casual thing to me," Adam told her. "This is special, maybe once-in-a-lifetime special."

"You can't know that—" Emma protested.

"Yes, I can," Adam said steadily. "You may as well know I'm not going to give up on you, Kurt or no Kurt. I'd like to fly out to Sunset Island and visit you—soon."

"Oh, no," Emma protested. "Kurt's on the island. It would break his heart!"

"What about *your* heart, Emma?" Adam asked.

"God, I don't know!" Emma cried, burying her head in her hands.

"You don't have to figure it out right now," Adam told her, stroking her hair. "Just think about it." He stood up and lifted her from the chair. Seeing the tears on her face, he gently wiped them away. "You wouldn't be crying if you didn't care about me," he said.

"I know," she whispered, gulping hard.

He pulled Emma gently toward him. Then wordlessly, they headed backstage where everyone was waiting. And Emma realized that for the first time that evening, Adam wasn't holding her hand.

"I'm still hungry," Sam told Emma and Carrie, reaching for the last crumbs of chips leftover in the bowl. "Want to get more room service?"

"Sam, it's almost three o'clock in the morning," Carrie pointed out. "There is no more room service."

"Okay, I'll just raid the service bar again," Sam said, and walked across the room to forage for junk food.

The three girls had been talking ever since they arrived back at the hotel from the concert. They'd talked about Sam's relationship with her birth mother, about Carrie's letter to Josh, and about Emma's attraction to Adam.

But I haven't told them what's really going on between Adam and me, Emma thought to herself miserably. *I can't bring myself to tell them—they'd lose all respect for me—just like I'm losing all respect for myself.*

"They way I see it," Sam said, reaching for a can of mixed nuts, "is that until such time as you're married or engaged, you might as well enjoy the flirtation!"

"I don't know," Emma sighed.

"You're being too hard on yourself," Carrie told Emma. "It's not like you actually did anything with Adam!"

"Uh-huh," Emma mumbled, staring at the carpet. She hated herself for lying and couldn't bring herself to look Carrie in the eye.

"I mean, even after you get married you

can be attracted to other men!" Carrie said earnestly.

"Yeah," Sam agreed, picking out some cashews to pop into her mouth. "You just don't get to act on it anymore—which sounds like a total drag."

"It's not a drag to be faithful if you're really in love," Carrie said firmly. "Right, Em?"

"Well, it was difficult for you with Billy and Josh," Emma pointed out, wanting desperately to get away from the subject of her own fidelity.

"True," Carrie agreed. "But I was trying to hold on to the past, which is Josh. Kurt is your present and probably your future!"

"Well, as far as I'm concerned, two guys for every girl is a perfect arrangement," Sam stated.

"Oh yeah?" Carrie asked. "Then how come you get so jealous when Pres flirts with another girl?"

"I said two guys for every girl, not two girls for every guy!" Sam said with exasperation. "Anybody want some nuts?" She held the can out to her friends.

"You're not nearly as tough as you pretend," Carrie said.

"It's not really so different from how you're feeling about having two mothers," Emma pointed out, happy to get away from the subject of boys altogether.

"How do you figure?" Sam asked, sprawling in an oversized chair.

"Well, your loyalties feel torn, don't they?" Emma asked. "It's not so different."

"You have a point," Sam agreed. "I like Susan, but I feel kind of . . . I don't know . . . guilty liking her, you know?"

Carrie nodded. "As if you're being disloyal to your real mom."

"Right," Sam agreed. "I can't think of Susan as my mother. And then there's Carson . . ."

"He's a strange one, all right," Carrie said.

"I can't figure him out," Sam mused. "He seems so cold, and Susan's such a warm person. Don't they seem like an odd couple?"

"Like Kurt and me," Emma blurted out.

"Oh no," Carrie protested. "You guys are perfect together!"

"But we're opposites, just like Susan and Carson!"

"I don't know what he's really like," Sam

said. "Maybe he's Mr. Charming when I'm not around. Maybe he just hates me!"

"Maybe he's afraid that Susan is still in love with your birth father," Emma said thoughtfully.

"How could he?" Sam asked. "Susan hasn't even seen my birth father since before I was born!"

"Emma has a point," Carrie said. "Maybe seeing you just reminds him of how she had this torrid love affair with another guy."

"Great," Sam groaned. "That means he's going to hate me forever."

Torrid love affair with another guy. Emma repeated the phrase in her mind. *How could I do it? How can I ever tell Kurt the truth, when I can't even admit it to my very best friends?*

"You guys," Emma began, "I have to tell you something."

"What?" Carrie said, and then yawned widely. "God, I'm beat. I've got to get some sleep."

"Oh nothing," Emma said, losing her nerve. "It can wait."

"Good, because I'm fading fast," Carrie

said, standing up to stretch. "See you to-morrow."

Carrie took the elevator downstairs to the eleventh floor where her own room was located. She walked down the corridor to room 1112, slid the card-key into the door and the door opened. She went inside and flipped on the lights. And screamed.

There was a man in her room, standing at the window, looking out into the night.

He turned around so Carrie could see his face.

It was Josh.

TEN

"What the hell are you doing here?!" Carrie yelled, fighting back tears of fright. "You scared me to death."

"I came to see you," Josh said simply.

"What are you talking about?" Carrie yelled, the adrenaline rushing through her. "How the hell did you get into my room?"

"I saw Claudia Templeton downstairs, and she got hotel security to let me in. I told her you were expecting me."

"That's a total lie!" Carrie exclaimed.

"I know," Josh agreed, "but it worked."

"You have a hell of a lot of nerve, Josh," Carrie said, wearily sitting on her bed. "Do you know you scared the life out of me!"

"I know, and I'm sorry, but it seemed like the best way. You said in your letter you were going to be in San Francisco, so . . ." Josh put out his hands as if to add "here I am."

"So what?" Carrie interrupted. "I feel like I'm in some bad movie!" Carrie exclaimed.

"Give me ten minutes to talk with you," Josh said, his voice steely. "Then, if you want me to leave, I'll go and you'll never have to speak with me again if you don't want to."

Carrie pushed her hair out of her face wearily. "Isn't flying all the way out here a bit melodramatic?"

"No more melodramatic than getting a kiss-off letter from you after all these years," Josh said bitterly.

"Oh Josh, it wasn't a kiss-off letter," Carrie said earnestly. "We haven't been a couple in a long time."

"Yeah, but you've still hung on, haven't you," Josh pointed out. "And as long as you hung on, I hung on."

Carrie didn't say anything. She knew there was an element of truth to what Josh said.

He sat down on the other bed and stared at Carrie.

"Okay, let's have it," Carrie finally said.

"I got your letter," he said evenly.

"So you said," Carrie nodded.

"You're allowed to break up with me," he continued.

"I know that," Carrie said. "You said there was someone else and I decided it was only fair for me to let go—"

"But I think it's incredibly chicken of you to do it by letter," Josh said, "after all the time we've had together and all the things we've done. I mean, you were the first girl—the only girl—I ever slept with!"

Carrie nodded again, feeling more miserable by the second.

"So," Josh continued, "if it's really over, if you're not going to dance around anymore like there could be a future for us, you're going to have to look me in the eye and say so to my face. Here's your chance."

Carrie looked at him and a wave of emotion overcame her. *I've known Josh since I was really just a girl. We've done a million things together. He loves me completely. Look! He's not rich, and he put himself on a plane to come out here and see me, to see if I'd take him back. What an effort. He's such a terrific guy. Was I wrong to send him that letter?* But no, this time, finally, she knew what she had to do.

"Josh," Carrie said, "you mean a lot to me."

"I know that," he said. "That's why I came out. That's why I can't believe you're just going to throw away everything we've had—we have," he corrected himself.

"It's not the same anymore," Carrie said. "You've changed; I've changed. Things have changed." *Boy, this sounds like every bad television show I've ever seen,* Carrie couldn't help thinking. *And I'm playing the lead role.*

"What's changed?" Josh demanded. "Tell me one damn thing that's changed! My feelings haven't changed. We've gotten a little older, that's true, but we've got something really special, and I think you're about to throw it away."

Carrie sat quietly for a moment. "There's Billy," she finally said.

"Yeah, Billy," Josh repeated with disgust.

"I love him," Carrie said simply.

"Look, you told me that before, Carrie, when I came to visit you," Josh reminded her.

"Well, that hasn't changed," Carrie said honestly.

"It's a summer romance!" Josh said. "It happens! It's like being on a cruise ship and falling in love—you're in this artificial environment where nothing ever goes wrong, and—"

"That's not true, Josh," Carrie said. "I really care about him."

"And he really cares about you, I'm sure," Josh said seriously. "All I'm saying is that you're betting on him instead of on me, and I think I'm a much better bet. He wouldn't fly out in the middle of the night to try to get you back. I'm sure of that."

He may be right about Billy on that score, at least the Billy I know so far. But who knows what the future will bring? There's no easy way out of this, Carrie thought, sitting silently on the bed. *Who's wrong and who's right? How do you know when you make the right decision, when you won't know the results of it for a long time?*

Finally, Carrie mustered up all her courage and spoke.

"Josh, you mean a lot to me," she said.

"You said that before," he replied, looking directly at her.

"I said that because it's true. And I hope that someday we'll be friends and be able to look back on this night and laugh about it—"

"Carrie, that's never gonna happen," Josh said sadly.

"No, I guess it isn't," Carrie agreed, fighting back tears. "But I'm ready to say it to your face. It's over."

Josh's face turned white. More than anything, Carrie wanted to reach out and comfort him, but she knew she couldn't do that. She was the one inflicting the pain.

"Then it's over," Josh said, with a note of finality in his voice. Carrie nodded again. Josh stood up.

"I guess I'll be going," he murmured. "I'm not sorry I came out here. I am sorry it ended this way."

Carrie nodded again. "Me too," she said. "It's my fault. Look, where are you going now? It's the middle of the night. There are two beds here. You can sleep in one of them."

"I think that would be worse than leaving," Josh said sadly. "No, I'll sleep in the waiting room at the airport or something."

"Are you sure?" Carrie asked, standing up.

"Uh-huh," Josh mumbled. He picked up a small backpack and walked to the door. Carrie followed him.

"Carrie Alden." Josh said, just as he was about to go.

"Yes?" Carrie said softly.

"Nothing," Josh said, "I just like to say your name."

Then they were in each other's arms, and Carrie smelled the familiar good smell of Josh's cologne, and she almost changed her mind about his leaving.

But she didn't. Josh was out the door. Carrie fell back on her bed and cried as if her heart were breaking, because it was.

Emma looked at the luminous dials of the clock near the bed and groaned. It had been around three o'clock when Carrie left and she'd finally gotten into bed. Now it was a little after four, and she hadn't slept a wink.

Adam. Kurt. Adam. Kurt. The two names kept repeating over and over in her mind. Images of Adam, the feel of his kisses, kept coming back to her. *I'm a whole other person with Adam,* she thought. *That person just wants to run away with him to Africa or to a movie set or—well, just away!* Emma thought wildly.

Then she thought of Kurt back on Sunset Island, who'd be awake soon—the sun was already rising in Maine on the other side of the continent—and a wave of guilt swept over her again. *I love Kurt! I really love him! How can this be happening to me?*

"Go to sleep," she told herself out loud, and then turned the pillow over, snuggling her head back into the softness. But as soon as she closed her eyes, it was Adam's face she saw, Adam's hands she felt, Adam's lips . . .

Emma heard a rapping noise on the door to her suite. She sat up quickly, her heart pounding in her chest. *Who could it be?* She waited a moment, to make sure she'd actually heard what she thought she'd heard.

Knock-knock-knock.

There it was again. *It's probably Carrie, she told herself, she's just too excited to sleep. Just like me. Good, I'm glad she's there. I could use someone to talk to. I've got*

a lot to talk about. And Carrie's so reason-
able and mature, she'll know just what to
do.

Emma got out of bed, and dressed in the oversized T-shirt she slept in, went to the door.

"Who is it?" she said, peering through the peephole.

"It's me," came a low voice.

It wasn't Carrie out there. It was Adam.

Before she could think or stop herself or worry about the consequences, Emma opened the door. She and Adam were instantly in each other's arms.

"I tried to stay away," he whispered into her hair. "I couldn't. . . ."

Instead of the words scaring her, Emma felt a wild thrill race through her. It was a powerful feeling, to know she had this much effect on this wonderful guy. But even as she kissed him back, Emma felt the danger, and the conflict, overcome the passion.

"Adam, we can't do this. . . ." Emma whispered.

"We don't have to make love," Adam said, kissing her neck. "I just want to be with you."

For just a moment, Emma closed her eyes and let the blissful feeling of Adam's kisses take over. *It would be so easy to just let it happen,* Emma thought. *So easy . . .*

But then she thought about Kurt, and how she'd decided to take things slowly, how she'd promised him that when she was ready, it would be with him that she'd share that experience. It just couldn't happen like this, here, now. But being alone in a hotel room with Adam was too dangerous. Emma wasn't sure she could keep her body from overruling her brain.

"Adam," Emma said breathlessly, "let's get out of here."

"But we can be alone here," Adam murmured, wrapping his arms around her narrow waist.

"I know," Emma replied. "It's too . . . I'm not . . ."

"I understand," Adam said with a sigh. "Where do you want to go?"

To Paris, to the moon, to the ends of the earth, to the asteroid B-612, anywhere as long as you're there! Emma wanted to scream. But instead she said "How about back to the beach at the Cliff House? I liked it there."

"I've got a better idea. Baker Beach," he said. "Put on some clothes and we can be there in fifteen minutes."

"Okay," Emma said. She went into the bathroom and came out wearing a Goucher College sweatsuit. "How's this?" she asked.

"Very hot," Adam said. "But I think you'd look hot in a green bell-bottom polyester pantsuit." They both laughed, and Adam reached for her again.

"Come on," Emma said, leading Adam to the door. "If we don't leave now we might never leave."

As the door closed behind her, Emma breathed an enormous sigh of relief. She looked over at Adam as they walked down the hall. *I'm going to live for right now, just this once,* she told herself.

A half hour later, Emma and Adam were curled up together under a blanket on Baker Beach, which Emma could see was just to the west of the Golden Gate Bridge on the San Francisco side of the bay. They could hear the late-night traffic rolling by on the bridge.

"We're lucky," Adam said, holding Emma

tight. "A lot of times this beach is covered in fog. Not tonight, though."

"Yes," Emma murmured, "not tonight." She snuggled against him.

"Do you have any idea how I feel about you right now?" Adam asked suddenly.

"You like me a lot?" Emma ventured.

"Worse than that," Adam said. "What you said to me tonight about that guy back on Sunset Island only made me want you more. I'm on a quest for you—you're my Dulcinea."

Dulcinea—that's the heroine from Don Quixote *by Cervantes,* Emma remembered. *Adam is alluding to Cervantes. Imagine a guy who's read Cervantes. How romantic can you get?*

"I'll settle for being just Emma," Emma said, trying against her will to put a lid on her emotions, "and we both know that I shouldn't be here."

"But you're here," Adam insisted.

"But I shouldn't be," Emma replied.

"I can accept that," Adam responded, curling up even more closely around Emma. "So long as you don't leave."

Oh hell, Emma thought. *I give up.* "I'm not going anywhere," Emma murmured.

"I know that," Adam said, his voice a little cocky.

"How can you be so confident?" Emma said, turning to face him.

"I drove," he said simply, "and the car keys are in my pocket."

"Oh you!" Emma said, and kissed Adam gently on the lips.

"What would you say if I told you that I love you?" Adam said to Emma, after the kiss.

"Don't say that!" Emma said quickly, warning bells going off in her head. "You don't even know me."

"Don't you believe in love at first sight?" Adam asked her.

"Not really," Emma said. "Not for me, anyway." But in the back of her mind she was wondering if this was what Darcy's dream had been about.

"Well," Adam said softly, looking into Emma's eyes carefully, "what would you call what's going on right now, right here, between you and me?"

Emma was silent for a moment. "I don't know what I'd call it," she finally said, "but I like it and I hate it at the same time. And it's scaring me half to death."

"That's the answer I was looking for," Adam said with a smile. "Let's hang out here a few more minutes, then I'll drive you back to the hotel." Emma nodded her assent, and the two of them lay together, curled against one another. They listened to the Pacific surf crash against the shore, like they were the only two people on the planet.

Two hours later, Emma could see the light of dawn through the hotel corridor windows as she walked to her room. She wasn't alone—Adam walked beside her. *I'm going to let him give me a good-night kiss, then I'm going to say good-night and go into my room—alone—and go to sleep. Finally.*

Emma put her key-card in the door and the lock opened. She went inside. Adam followed her. She turned to him.

"Kiss me good-night," she said softly, "then you have to go."

Without a word, he kissed her. Somehow as the kiss continued, they moved to Emma's bed.

"Adam?" Emma said softly.

"Yes?" Adam responded, gently caressing her cheek with the tips of his fingers.

"I'm not ready to sleep with you, or anybody, for that matter," she confessed.

"It's fine," Adam said.

"It is?" Emma responded.

"Yes," Adam said. "Timing is everything. I think I once heard Billy Joel say that."

Emma laughed, remembering Billy Joel's conversation with Ian Templeton earlier that evening. *Had it really been that same evening? So much has happened,* Emma thought.

"I'm really tired," Emma said, resting her head on his shoulder.

"Me too," Adam said, putting his arm around her.

Slowly, he lowered both of them down onto the bed, and with his arm around Emma and her head on his chest, they both fell fast asleep.

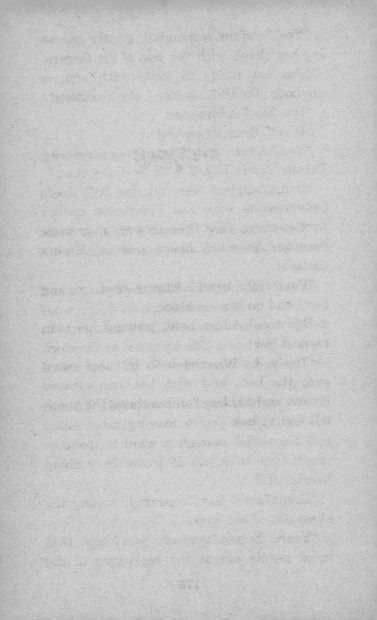

ELEVEN

"Good morning!" Susan's chipper voice rang out over the phone and into Sam's ear.

It was the morning after the concert, and Sam had been sound asleep having a wonderful dream about one of the guitarists in Billy Joel's band. She squinted at the clock by the bed. "What time is it?" she asked groggily.

"It's eight-thirty," Susan said. "I know it's early, but you're leaving later today and I'm selfish enough to want to spend as much time with you as I can. How about breakfast?"

"Breakfast?" Sam repeated, wiping the sleep out of her eyes.

"Yeah," Susan laughed, "you know, that meal people eat at the beginning of the day. I'm taking off work to spend the day with you until you leave," she added.

"Oh, well that's great," Sam said, beginning to feel semi-awake.

"I want to take you someplace amazing," Susan said.

"Not the Grand Piano again," Sam said, mock-grimacing. "I might end up leaving San Francisco with love beads around my neck."

"Hey, don't knock 'em!" Susan joked. "I still have mine from the sixties and I think they're hip again!"

"It's hard to picture you back then," Sam mused.

"I'll give you photographic evidence sometime," Susan said. "But if you laugh at my bell-bottoms you're dead meat!"

"No guarantees," Sam warned her jokingly.

"So look, I'll bring breakfast," Susan said, "and I'll pick you up in an hour."

Sam showered and dressed quickly in jeans, a men's white T-shirt and the leather bomber jacket with Minnie Mouse on the back. Then she took the elevator downstairs, where Susan was waiting, as usual, right on time.

"So where are we going?" Sam asked, as they got into Susan's Volvo.

"North," Susan answered mysteriously.

"Gee, that narrows it down," Sam allowed.

In a matter of minutes, they were headed across the Golden Gate Bridge towards Marin County, and Sam was shocked to see that the bridge was entirely swathed in the thickest fog she'd ever seen.

"Is this common, this fog?" Sam asked, a little concerned. "How can you see?"

"In the summer it's typical, and barely is how I can see," Susan answered as she squinted out the windshield, flicking on her low-beam headlights. "Best weather here is in October. But one good thing is that no one needs air–conditioning."

They drove in silence for a while on the Marin County side of the bridge. The weather cleared quickly after Susan exited from the highway. They turned onto an incredibly twisty road right along the coast. Sam stared out the window in amazement at the sheer cliffs leading down to the Pacific Ocean, and at the rolling hills covered by what looked like some kind of brush. She looked up and saw red-tailed hawks flying across the sky.

Then Susan turned off the winding road and followed a sign that read "To Muir Woods National Monument." She drove down a two-lane road for a while and then pulled into a parking lot.

"We're here," Susan said.

"We're here?" Sam repeated, looking around. "There's no here, here!"

"You'll see," Susan promised. "Follow me."

Sam walked down a paved path past some kind of visitor center with Susan at her side. *Hmmm. This is pretty ordinary,* Sam thought. *A nice forest.* Then Sam looked up. And all of a sudden she felt very, very small. They were walking under the biggest trees that Sam had ever seen. Redwood trees. Reaching skyward for hundreds of feet.

Susan, walking along next to Sam and carrying a small knapsack, seemed to sense Sam's feelings. "Feeling a little overwhelmed?" she asked Sam quietly.

Sam nodded.

"It happens to everyone who comes here," Susan said. "These trees are hundreds of years old. People come and go, countries come and go, and these trees just keep on growing."

"Wow," Sam said. She'd never seen anything like this. She wished Carrie was with her—*Emma's probably been here five or six times—she probably knows each tree's nickname,* she thought with a small smile.

"After World War II, when the United Nations was getting organized, but before they signed the treaty in San Francisco, they brought all the delegates out here for a walk," Susan said. "Something about humility."

"No kidding," Sam agreed, still staring up at the amazing trees.

"Hungry?" Susan asked.

"Always," Sam told her.

"Then let's stop and eat," Susan said, setting a basket onto a nearby picnic table. "Unfortunately we can't stay that long, because I've got to get you back to the hotel before your flight."

Susan spread out a small tablecloth, and on it she put four bagels, cream cheese, smoked salmon, fruit salad, a big knife, some paper napkins, and a thermos of coffee. For a while, Sam and she ate contently under the big trees. It was remarkably quiet. Then Sam spoke.

"Susan, why does Carson hate me?"

"I don't think he hates you," Susan said carefully.

"Okay," Sam allowed. "How about dislikes me intensely?"

Susan sighed. "What if I told you that I'm not sure I know the answer to that question?" she said finally.

"What if I told you I thought you weren't telling me something?" Sam replied.

"It wouldn't be the first time you said that," Susan pointed out, staring out into the distance. "Well, I think part of it," Susan continued, "is that he's threatened by you."

"Threatened?" Sam thought this was the strangest thing she'd ever heard. *How can Samantha Bridges threaten anyone?* she thought. *I'm not even famous yet.*

"Yes," Susan said. "It's like he's in competition with you for my attention, now."

"That's ridiculous."

"I'm not saying it's right or wrong," Susan said. "It's just how I think he must feel. He doesn't want to have to compete with you."

"You think that's it?" Sam asked.

"There's more to it than that," Susan admitted. "I also think that he thinks you're like a bad dream coming back to haunt him."

A bad dream. Me, a bad dream. Well, that makes me feel just grand. "Look," Sam said, hurt, "he can think what he wants. I'm not exactly crazy about him either."

"I don't blame you," Susan said softly. "But please believe me, the Carson you see is not who he really is."

"So who is he, really?" Sam asked skeptically.

"He's . . . a kind, fair, good person," Susan said earnestly. "And a wonderful father."

"Susan, with all due respect, that doesn't sound very romantic," Sam opined.

"Well, marriage isn't necessarily about romance," Susan said softly.

"Well, then I'm never getting married!" Sam announced, taking a final bite of fruit salad.

"Never say never," Susan counseled. "It can get you into a lot of trouble."

"I bet if you'd married Michael, it would have been romantic," Sam insisted.

"Well, that's a bet we'll never be able to

settle," Susan said, staring up at a giant tree. "But try to understand: For Carson, seeing you must be a reminder of my love for Michael—and my unfaithfulness to him."

"So am I supposed to pay for that?" Sam asked bitterly. "I didn't ask to be born!"

"No, you didn't," Susan agreed. She turned to Sam and touched her hand. "I asked for you to be born."

Sam bit her lower lip as emotions assailed her. "Are you . . . are you glad?" she whispered.

"Sam, you are one of the greatest blessings of my life," Susan said simply.

Carrie woke up around ten o'clock, with her eyes burning and a bad dream about Josh in her mind. *Was he really here last night? Did I really and truly break up with him once and for all? Did he actually fly here from the East Coast?* Then Carrie's eyes lit on a copy of the *New York Times* that had been left on the windowsill. She knew that she hadn't bought it and she knew that Josh had really been there.

Why do I feel so horrible when I know I did the right thing? Carrie asked herself as she got out of bed. *I've got to talk to someone. Emma—she'll be awake; she always gets up early.*

She pulled on a pair of jeans and a Yale sweatshirt, and with her feet still bare, took the elevator up to Emma's floor.

At Emma's suite, she rapped on the door.

"Just a sec!" came Emma's voice. "It's room service," Carrie heard Emma mumble to herself. "I'll be right there!"

The door to the room swung open. Carrie saw Emma dressed in an oversized T-shirt standing at the door. Then Carrie looked past Emma into the room.

And there, in Emma's bed, was Adam.

"Carrie! This isn't what it looks like," Emma said quickly.

"I, uh . . ." Carrie stammered. "Look, I can leave—"

"No, don't," Emma interrupted. She looked over at Adam.

"Maybe this would be a good time for me to be going," Adam said, getting out of bed.

Although Carrie averted her eyes, when Adam got up she saw that he still had his jeans on. *Big deal,* she said to herself as she looked everywhere except at Adam. *He was still in Emma's bed!*

"I'll come back in a few hours to take you

183

guys to the airport," Adam said as he hastily finished dressing. He kissed Emma and then gave Carrie a departing grin. "Enjoy my half of the room service!" he said, and was out the door.

"Well, I feel like the hind end of a donkey," Carrie said.

"Sit down," Emma said wearily. "And I'm the one who should feel like an ass."

"I didn't mean to barge in on anything," Carrie insisted.

"You didn't know there was anything to barge in on," Emma pointed out, sitting on the other bed.

"True," Carrie agreed, still feeling a little dazed by what she'd just seen. "I . . . uh . . . came up to talk to you about a problem. About Josh."

"You're going to talk to me about a problem with a guy?" Emma laughed bitterly, "I'm just the girl to give you advice and support. Don't you want to know what Adam was doing in bed with me?!" Emma was on the verge of tears.

"Well, yeah," Carrie admitted. "But that's up to you. You'll tell me when you're ready," she said simply.

"We didn't make love," Emma said defensively.

"Emma, you don't have to defend yourself to me just because I barged in here—"

"I'm not," Emma said. "I'm . . . oh, God, I don't know what I am."

"Well, join the club," Carrie said. "I don't know what I am, either, other than confused. You're not going to believe this, but Josh was here last night."

"Josh!?" Emma repeated, temporarily forgetting her own predicament.

There was a loud knock on the door.

"And I suppose that's him now," Emma joked.

"I have a feeling it's your room service," Carrie said dryly.

Emma opened the door and a waiter wheeled in the breakfast. She signed for it quickly and he left.

"Are you serious?" Emma asked, pouring them each a cup of tea.

"Yep," Carrie said, too tired to show much emotion. "He was waiting in my room when I got there."

"You're kidding," Emma said. "You're just saying this to make me feel better."

"Emma, I swear this is the truth," Carrie

said. And she told Emma about why Josh had flown out to San Francisco from New Jersey, how he had gotten into her room and how they had broken up once and for all.

"So that's that," Carrie concluded. "He slept in the airline terminal last night, I guess."

"What are you going to tell Billy?" Emma asked.

"I don't know. What are you going tell Kurt?" Carrie asked.

"Hey girlfriends!" Sam breezed in the door without knocking. "Susan took me to the most incredible place this morning and . . . hey, why the long faces?" Sam looked from Carrie to Emma and back to Carrie again. Neither of them seemed to be able to look her in the eye.

"Josh came last night," Carrie finally said.

"I spent last night sleeping with your brother," Emma said.

"April Fool!" Sam yelled out joyously, bounding around the room. "You guys fooled me completely, I'll tell you, and—" Sam stopped laughing. Neither Emma nor Carrie had cracked even a tiny smile.

"C'mon," Sam said, "joke's over!" Emma and Carrie just looked at her.

"You mean it's true? Nah. Really?" Carrie and Emma nodded.

"Whoa, baby," Sam said, whistling a low whistle. "This is great stuff. Tell me every sordid detail!"

"It's not funny, Sam," Emma said. "Ever since I saw your brother Adam I've had the most incredible crush on him. I haven't felt this way since I was about thirteen. We've spent the last two nights making out on the beach, and last night, he slept right here! We didn't make love," she added quickly.

"I could see him looking at you," Sam replied, "but I thought it was just your natural charm."

"I feel so awful!" Emma said, tears coming to her eyes. "Like a total cheat. I've completely betrayed Kurt."

"May I remind you that once Kurt completely betrayed you," Sam said, referring to the time Kurt had gone to New York with Diana De Witt. "And in his case, he really did sleep with her!"

"Yes, and if you recall, I broke up with

him over it!" Emma exclaimed. "Anyway, two wrongs don't make a right."

"Maybe not," Sam shrugged. "Anyway, you didn't do anything so awful. And besides, Kurt doesn't have to know," Sam added, sitting down on the edge of Emma's bed.

"Of course he does!" Emma insisted. "I have to tell him!"

"No, you don't," Sam replied. "Now what's this about Josh? He suddenly materialized here like out of *Star Trek?*"

For the second time in an hour, Carrie recounted the story of Josh's visit to San Francisco and how she had finally called it quits with him.

"I know it was the right thing to do," Carrie concluded, "but it still hurts so much. Josh really loves me. . . ."

"And Kurt really loves me," Emma said with anguish, "and now I've ruined it!"

"You haven't ruined anything," Sam said. "Two guys for every girl. That's what I say. It's Carrie who's ruined the ratio."

But neither Emma nor Carrie thought Sam was the least bit funny. They both looked completely miserable.

"I'm sorry you're both feeling so bad,"

Sam said, all levity gone from her voice. "I wish I knew the right thing to say so you'd feel better."

"Just having you guys as friends helps," Carrie said, gulping hard. "I know I'll get over this terrible ache in my heart . . . eventually. It's just so hard to know that I hurt someone I really care about."

"At least you know you did the right thing," Emma said, tears spilling down her cheeks. "You wanted Josh to be free. But I love Kurt, and I don't want to let go of him. I've hurt him for no good reason at all!"

Carrie and Sam both moved to comfort Emma, who couldn't stop crying.

"I hate myself!" Emma wailed.

"It'll be okay," Carrie crooned, patting Emma on the back. "Kurt loves you. He'll understand."

But though Carrie said it, none of the girls was convinced it was true.

TWELVE

"I had a wonderful time," Sam told Susan. They were standing at the departure gate. The plane was about ready to be boarded. Emma was standing a ways away from them, talking earnestly with Adam. Carrie was in some VIP room with Graham, Claudia and the kids, ready to be whisked onto the plane at the last minute.

"I had a wonderful time, too," Susan said, reaching up to hug Sam. "God, it's amazing that I have a daughter this tall," she joked.

Daughter. It still sounded so strange to Sam. At that moment she missed her real mother with a sudden fierceness. *I'll call her as soon as I get back to the island,* she promised herself.

"I know it's silly," Susan said, "but I miss you already."

"I'll write," Sam promised.

Susan laughed. "I won't hold my breath. You aren't the world's greatest correspondant."

"Well, I'll try," Sam amended.

Susan stared lovingly at Sam. "At the risk of sounding hopelessly mushy, I just want to say . . . I know Michael would have been very proud of you."

"What if he's not dead?" Sam blurted out.

"What?" Susan echoed, obviously taken aback.

"What if he's not dead?" she asked again. "I'm sorry, Susan, I told myself not to bring it up, but . . ."

"I think there's very little chance that he's alive, Sam," Susan said gently.

"You should have told him about me when you had the chance!" San insisted.

"Maybe," Susan agreed, her voice steady. "But then, hindsight is always twenty-twenty."

"I just wish . . ." Sam began, her voice trailing off.

"I know," Susan said. "I wish it, too."

"American Airlines Flight 407 to Boston, with continuing service to Portland will now begin boarding," came a female voice over the intercom system.

"Well, I guess this is it," Susan said. "I hope you'll visit again as soon as possible."

Sam lifted her carry-on bag, then put it down again. "Do you have their address?" she asked suddenly.

"Whose?" Susan queried.

"Michael Blady's parents—you said they wrote to you."

A guarded look came over Susan's face. "Why would you want that?"

"I want to tell them they have a granddaughter," Sam said simply.

"Oh, I don't know. . . ." Susan began.

"But you do have it?" Sam pressed. "Their address in Israel?"

"I do," Susan admitted.

"Will you send it to me?"

Susan rubbed her hand anxiously across her forehead. "I don't know—"

"Will you think about it? Please?"

Susan took a deep breath and finally nodded. "I'll think about it. Oh, I almost forgot!" Susan exclaimed, reaching into her oversized bag and pulling out a package wrapped in gold foil. "This is for you."

"Thanks!" Sam said, and turned it over to pull at the tape.

"No," Susan said quickly. "Open it on the plane."

"Okay," Sam said, shoving the present into the side pocket of her carry-on bag. "Listen, I appreciate whatever it is, but honestly, what I'd really like is that address in Israel."

"Michael's parents might even be dead by now," Susan said quietly.

"Maybe," Sam allowed, "but maybe not. I have the right to find out."

"This is a final boarding call for American Airlines flight 407 to Boston," the voice announced over the intercom.

"Well, I guess this is good-bye," Emma told Adam in a tight voice.

"It's not good-bye, Emma," Adam insisted. "It can't just end like this."

"It has to!" Emma cried. "I can't stand this! I feel torn in two!"

"Look. You didn't plan for me to come into your life, but I did, and you can't change that now," Adam said, brushing a strand of hair gently from Emma's face.

"I don't know," Emma moaned miserably. "I just don't know. . . ."

"Can I call you?" Adam asked.

"No!" Emma said firmly.

"Just a phone call—"

"No!" she repeated. "I've got to have time to think, to decide—"

"I can help you decide—"

"Adam, no," she said. "I mean it. I'll call you when I'm ready."

"When?" Adam asked. "A day from now? A week?"

"I don't know," Emma replied. "I'm not playing games or hard to get or being coy," she explained earnestly. "You'll just have to accept that right now I don't know."

Adam was silent for a moment. "Okay," he finally said. "But, like I said, I'm not giving up on you." He took her in his arms, and for the last time Emma felt the thrill of his lips on hers.

"I've got to go," she whispered, her eyes filling with tears. She broke away from him.

"Emma—" Adam called, reaching out for her.

But she ran for the plane and didn't dare look back.

* * *

An hour later, Carrie made her way back to the coach section of the plane. She found Emma staring past an older woman in the window seat out into the clouds and Sam staring straight ahead into space.

"Hi," she said, balancing on Sam's armrest. "Want to come invade the front of the plane? There're a bunch of empty seats up there. No one will care."

Sam shrugged and Emma didn't even seem to hear her.

"Are you guys okay?" Carrie asked.

"I'm just thinking," Sam said absently.

"Emma?" Carrie asked.

Emma snapped her head towards Carrie. "What?"

"I asked if you were okay," Carrie said.

"Not really," Emma whispered honestly.

"You want to talk about it?" Carrie asked.

Emma sighed and her eyes filled with tears again. "I just don't know what to do!" she cried.

"Excuse me," the woman next to her said in a heavy New York accent. "I don't mean to be a big buttinsky, but a good talk always helps. I swear to Gawd."

196

Emma looked at the woman as if she were staring at roadkill that had suddenly found the power of speech.

"Everyone confides in me," the woman continued, the dozen bracelets on her arm jangling as she wiped at the corner of her lip-glossed mouth with a razor-sharp red fingernail. "How do you stop lip gloss from creeping over the lip-line? This is something I'd kill to know," she sighed.

"Excuse me, madam," Emma said in her frostiest voice, "I don't recall addressing you."

"Well excuse me for living, why-doncha?" the woman whined, obviously offended.

"Hey, let's go up to the front of the plane and see Graham!" Carrie said in a perky voice, half lifting Sam and Emma from their seats.

"Graham Perry?" the woman yelled after them as they headed up the aisle. "I heard he was on this plane. I'm such a fan, I swear to Gawd . . ."

"Emma, you are too much," Sam laughed a few minutes later as she fell into one of the many empty seats in first class.

"I was a bitch," Emma said flatly, sitting

197

down next to her. "I shouldn't take my misery out on some stranger—"

"No, you shouldn't," Carrie agreed, "and it's not like you to, either."

Emma passed her hand over her eyes wearily. "I wish I could crawl into bed and pull the covers over my head. I wish this plane would never land!"

"Kurt's gonna be waiting for you at the airport, huh," Sam asked.

Emma nodded. "You know Billy and Pres are picking Kurt up in the van. God, I remember thinking how sweet it was that they were going to meet us, how much I was looking forward to seeing Kurt's face when I got off the airplane. . . ."

"Just remember what I told you," Sam said, dangling her long legs over the side of the seat. "You don't have to tell him."

"That's so dishonest!" Emma cried. "I can't do that! How would I live with myself?"

"Sam has a point," Carrie said slowly.

Emma looked at Carrie with shock. "I can't believe you're agreeing with her!"

"Well, I don't know if I am," Carrie qualified. "I'm just saying she has a point. I remember reading this magazine article by a family therapist. It was all about this happily married woman who went out of town on business, and she had this one-night-stand, and then when she came home she felt terrible, and she couldn't decide whether or not she should tell her husband."

"And?" Sam prompted.

"And the therapist said that telling the husband might make her feel less guilty, but it could really devastate her husband and harm her marriage. So instead of telling, the therapist suggested that the woman keep her mouth shut, but learn something from it—namely, why she had done it."

"So, you're saying I'd be telling Kurt the truth to assuage my own guilt instead of because it's the right thing to do?" Emma asked.

"Well, it's worth considering," Carrie said with a shrug.

"Can I get you girls anything to drink?" the flight attendant asked pleasantly.

"Do you mind if my friends are up here?" Carrie asked quickly.

"Not unless someone else minds," the

flight attendant said. "We're almost empty up here, anyway."

"I'll have a Coke," Sam said. "And maybe some peanuts?"

"Sure," the flight attendant said and headed for the galley.

"Maybe I should be a flight attendant," Sam mused, watching the girl walk away. "Seems easy enough, and I hear you get to fly all over practically for free."

"You'd wise off to the first rude guy who hit on you and it would be all over," Carrie said with a laugh.

"I guess you're right," Sam agreed. "Anyway, I'd rather be flying first class than waiting on people in first class."

"That's the Sam I know and love," Carrie agreed with a laugh.

Sam leaned close to Emma and touched her on the arm. "Em?"

Emma was startled out of her revery. "What?"

"Listen," Sam continued, "I know you're really bummed out about what happened, but it happened for a reason."

"Because I'm a fickle bitch?" Emma said bitterly.

"Of course not," Sam said. "I think it

happened because Kurt was coming on so strong right before you left the island. All of a sudden he was crowding you, and it freaked you out!"

"But I love Kurt!" Emma protested. "Why would that freak me out?"

"Because you're nineteen and a fox to the max!" Sam exclaimed. "Why would you want to give up your freedom now?"

"Or maybe," Carrie said slowly, "it's because it seemed like Kurt was getting more serious because he was afraid of losing you—you know—out of insecurity, instead of because you guys are ready for that step."

Emma thought for a moment. "I . . . I think that's right," she agreed. "It didn't feel like Kurt really wanted us to be engaged-to-be-engaged so much as he got scared!"

"Let's face it," Sam said smugly, "your two bestest buddies are totally brilliant."

"Here's your Coke," the flight attendant said, handing Sam the drink and a couple packs of nuts. "We'll be serving dinner shortly."

"Thanks," Sam said, tearing open a pack of nuts.

"You two definitely have a point," Emma said. "But I don't know that Adam was just some dumb fling. I don't feel like he was!"

"You're hot for my bro, huh?" Sam asked salaciously, pouring some nuts into her mouth. "Well, I can't say that I blame you. I could go for him myself. I mean, he's not really related to me by blood or anything, since he's adopted—"

"Try to stay focused on the subject, Sam," Carrie interrupted.

"What?" Sam asked innocently. "I thought the subject was Adam!"

Carrie ignored her and turned to Emma. "You really have feelings for him?"

"I think so," Emma admitted. "I just don't know!"

"Well, that does make it more complicated," Carrie admitted.

"Yeah, it's one thing to have a fling," Sam said, "and another to really fall for another guy."

"Are you going to see Adam again?" Carrie asked Emma.

"He wants to come to the island and visit me," Emma told them, "as soon as possible."

"Get out of here!" Sam exclaimed. "*Quelle conquest!*"

"What are you going to do?" Carrie wondered.

Emma stared out the window a moment. Then she turned back to her friends. "I'm going to write to Adam and tell him it's over," she finally said. "And I'm never going to see him again."

Carrie whistled softly under her breath. "You're sure?"

"No," Emma admitted. "I'm not sure of anything. But it's what I have to do."

"And are you going to tell Kurt about Adam?" Sam asked.

"I don't know," Emma said anxiously.

"Well, if it's any help at all," Carrie said, "now that I finally cut Josh loose, once and for all, I'm starting to feel less . . . conflicted, I guess is the word."

Emma nodded. "Right now I'm a complete mass of conflicts. But I'm hoping that when I see Kurt, I'll know the right thing to do."

After dinner both Carrie and Emma fell into an exhausted sleep, but Sam was restless and couldn't seem to relax. She

203

wandered back into the coach section to get a magazine out of her pack. When she unzipped the side of her bag, the first thing she saw was the gift Susan had given her before she got on the plane.

Well, no time like the present, Sam thought, and tore the paper off the package. Inside was a book entitled *They Survived* by Beth Davidson.

"Well, I guess that's what an editor gives for presents—books." Sam sighed, turning the book over in her hand. *Too bad Susan's not a fashion designer,* she added to herself.

And then it seemed as if Sam's heart stopped, because staring at her from the back of the book was a face that looked very, very much like her own.

"Hey, that looks just like you!" the woman from New York cried, leaning over practically into Sam's lap.

Sam pulled the book away, stood up, grabbed her bag and headed for the bathroom. Once she was inside she locked the door and sat down on the toilet to look at the book in private. She stared at the face again. Weird.

"Who the hell is Beth Davidson?" Sam

asked herself out loud. She opened the book and saw that Susan had scribbled something on the inside of the front cover. It read:

I GIVE YOU THIS BOOK AS PART OF YOUR JOURNEY IN DISCOVER- ING YOUR PAST. ALL MY LOVE, SUSAN.

"But what does it mean?" Sam whispered. She read the copy on the cover flap, and slowly, incredibly, it all made sense. "In this heart-felt odyssey, the author tells the story of her parents' life, from wealth and success in Norway to the death camp of Auschwitz. . . ."

And then Sam read the dedication: "To my beloved parents, Lillian and Joseph Blady, who survived."

Slowly, Sam turned the book over again and stared at the photo of a woman with wild, curly hair and a challenging look in her eyes. *My Aunt Beth,* Sam thought to herself, with pride and wonder. *I look like my Aunt Beth, who is an author.*

"Excuse me, miss, are you okay in there?" a flight attendant called in to her.

"Uh, yeah," Sam said, quickly stowing her book in her carry-on bag. She opened the bathroom door and headed toward the first-class section to be with her friends. Both Carrie and Emma were sound asleep. Sam found an empty row and spread out over the seats. Then she opened the book and began to read.

The plane landed in Boston for a brief stopover and then their flight continued on to Portland.

"This is your captain speaking," came the voice over the intercom. "We'll be landing in Portland in about five minutes, folks. The temperature is seventy-five degrees, with partly-cloudy skies. Thank you for flying with us on American."

"I can't wait to see Billy," Carrie said.

"Graham and Claudia don't mind that your boyfriend is meeting the plane?" Emma asked.

"I didn't exactly tell them," Carrie admitted, craning her neck up the aisle to where Graham, Claudia, Ian and Chloe were sitting. "But I figure one quick hug and kiss won't hurt—I just won't be able to go back in the van with you guys."

"Right now I don't want to go back at all," Emma said. "Maybe if I offer the pilot a big enough bribe he'll turn the plane around and head back for California," she suggested feebly.

"Would you rather be back there with Adam?" Carrie asked with surprise.

"No," Emma admitted, fastening her seat belt. "I just don't want to face Kurt."

"Well, your bucks can't buy you out of this one," Sam said philosophically.

"Hey, what was that book you had your head buried in, Sam?" Carrie asked. "It's the first time I ever saw you reading something longer than a magazine article."

"Oh, just a book Susan gave me," Sam said with a shrug. *This isn't the right time to tell them about it,* Sam decided. *Emma is all anxious about Kurt, and Carrie is totally preoccupied thinking about Billy. Besides, I need to keep it to myself for just a little while.*

The plane touched down and taxied to the gate, finally coming to a stop. The girls grabbed their things and stood up.

"Carrie, grab Chloe, will you?" Claudia called to her.

"Sure," Carrie said, reaching down to lift the little girl.

"Well, that's going to be a lovely addition to your greeting Billy," Sam said in Carrie's ear.

Carrie shrugged and sighed a what-can-I-do sigh and followed Sam and Emma off the plane.

Standing at the gate, looking incredibly cute, were Billy, Pres and Kurt.

"I'll just be a second!" Carrie called to Claudia, and she put Chloe down next to her. The next thing she knew she was wrapped in Billy's arms.

"You feel great," he murmured into her hair.

"I am so glad to see you," she told him.

"We have to go with Mommy and Daddy," Chloe said, pulling on Carrie's jeans anxiously.

"Sorry," Carrie sighed. "I'm working—I have to go."

"You can't go back with me?" Billy asked.

"Go back with him," Claudia said, coming up next to her. "I'll take Chloe."

"Are you sure?" Carrie asked. "I should have told you he was meeting the plane. . . ."

"Yes, you should have," Claudia agreed, "but it's okay. I'm beat and so is this little one. I'm sure she'll sleep in the limo anyway."

"Thanks Claudia," Carrie said gratefully.

"You can get up with her in the morning," Claudia called back to Carrie, and headed off with the little girl.

"So was it great?" Billy asked.

"So much happened to all of us," Carrie said, and she looked over at Sam, who was standing in front of Pres with a huge grin on her face.

"Girl, you are a sight for sore eyes," Pres drawled, and enveloped Sam in a bear hug.

"You're looking pretty fine, yourself," Sam told him, nuzzling into his arms. "Mmmmm," she added, sniffing his neck appreciatively. "You smell good, too."

"Well, dang, little darling, I up and decided to bathe, in honor of your homecoming and all," Pres said solemnly. He held her close and stroked her hair back off her face. "How was it?"

"Mostly wonderful," Sam said, "for me, anyway." And then she looked over at Emma.

"Emma," Kurt breathed. Then he held her wordlessly in his arms. "I missed you so much," he finally whispered. "I'm so glad you're home."

"Me too," Emma whispered, and she found that it was true. *I don't even know Adam,* she realized. *It almost feels like it was all a dream right now. Kurt is real.*

And she knew then what she had to do. *I don't know if it's the right thing to do or the wrong thing to do,* Emma said to herself, gulping hard over the knot in her throat, *but I know it's the only thing I can do.*

"You okay?" Sam called to her.

Emma nodded and attempted to smile, but her bottom lip started quivering. Sam moved out of Pres's arms and headed for her friend. At the same moment Carrie walked away from Billy and moved toward Emma and Sam.

Without a word, Sam and Carrie put their arms around Emma and hugged her tight.

"Thanks," Emma whispered.

"One for all and all for one," Sam reminded them.

"Always," Carrie affirmed.

They released each other and Carrie

walked back over to Billy, ready to tell him she'd broken up with Josh once and for all. Sam walked back to Pres, ready to share with him the incredible, scary journey she was on in discovering this new family. And Emma . . . Emma was ready to tell Kurt the truth. Whatever happened, she knew she'd be okay.

"Kurt," she said, looking him right in the eye, "there's something I have to tell you."

"What?" he asked, a hint of anxiety in his face.

"I love you very much," Emma said simply. She took Kurt's hand, smiled at Carrie and Sam, and the six of them walked on.

SUNSET ISLAND MAILBOX

Dear Readers,

Picture this—I'm at my computer writing the latest <u>Sunset Island</u> adventure. The fatter of my two cats, Trinity, is asleep on my desk, sort of blobbing over on to the keyboard. My husband comes in with a big envelope from my publisher—more mail from the incredibly cool, fabulous readers of Sunset Island!

I'm so psyched—I immediately read every single letter. And I answer them all, too—that's a promise. Just remember, if you want your letter considered for publication, say so. If you want a private response only, that's fine, too.

IMPORTANT NEWS FLASH! Many of you have written showing concern that now that my new series, <u>Sunset After Dark</u>, is debuting, I'll stop writing <u>Sunset Island</u> books. Hey, how could I possibly stop writing about Emma, Sam, and Carrie? Now you'll have both series to read.

As always, I love receiving your ideas, opinions, pictures—everything! I'll keep writing as long as you keep reading.

See you on the island!
Best—
Cherie Bennett

Cherie Bennett
c/o General Licensing Company, Inc.
24 West 25th Street
New York, New York 10010

Dear Cherie,

Sunset Island *books are the greatest!!! I never get tired of reading them. I have an idea for a future book. Sam could audition for a dancer's part in a Broadway play, and make the part. She could realize Broadway is not all it's cracked up to be, and quit and go back to Sunset Island.*

> *Your biggest fan,*
> *Sara Beth Kirby*
> *Wantagh, New York*

Dear Sara,

That's a terrific idea! What do the rest of you think? For those of you who like to think up story ideas for Sam, Emma, and Carrie, this summer you will be invited to enter them in a contest. The winning entry will be used as the basis of a future book, and the winner will be awarded a trip to Nashville to meet me. Watch for contest details in upcoming books!

> Best,
> Cherie

Dear Cherie,

I just got through reading Sunset Whispers. *It was fantastic! You caught my interest from the very first page. You said that you are a singer and live in Nashville, Tennessee, but you write about rock music. What kind of music do you sing?*

> *Your newest fan,*
> *Misty L. Sessions*
> *Rusk, Texas*

Dear Misty,

Actually, I'm not doing any singing right now because I'm too busy writing! And while I write mostly about rock music in Sunset Island, I write about country music, too. I wrote a play called <u>Honky Tonk Angels</u> for which Garth Brooks wrote all the songs. I'd love to know what singers all of you out there like and listen to. Let me know in a letter—maybe I can have that singer visit Sunset Island!

Best,
Cherie

Dear Cherie,

Hi! My name is Sarah Stanbro, and I'm sixteen years old. I'm a junior at Sonoma Valley High. I love reading your Sunset Island *books and I hope you keep the series going for years to come. I admire all the characters, but the thing I most admire about them is that they go after what they want with determination and they don't give up until they get it. It's made me realize that I, too, can do anything I set my mind to, and I want to thank you for showing me that.*

Sincerely,
Sarah Stanbro
Sonoma, California

Dear Sarah,

Your letter really made my day. I guess if there's one thing I'd like all of you to get out there (besides sharing in fun adventures) is that you really <u>can</u> make your dreams come true. Just as with Emma, Carrie, and Sam you will find obstacles in your life, yet you have the power within you to make things happen, to become the very best you that you can be. Reach for the stars!

Best,
Cherie